PASTIME

ROBERT B. PARKER

PASTIME

G. P. PUTNAM'S SONS NEW YORK

G. P. Putnam's Sons
Publishers Since 1838
200 Madison Avenue
New York, NY 10016

Library of Congress Cataloging-in-Publication Data

Parker, Robert B., date
Pastime / Robert B. Parker.
p. cm.
ISBN 0-399-13628-2 (acid-free paper)
ISBN 0-399-13630-4 (Limited Edition)
I. Title.
PS3566.A686P34 1991   91-8745 CIP
813'.54—dc20

Printed in the United States of America
1 2 3 4 5 6 7 8 9 10

This book is printed on acid-free paper.
∞

For my wife and sons—*sine qua non*

1

The dog was a pointer, a solid chocolate German Short-hair, three years old and smallish for her breed. She sat bolt upright on the couch in Susan Silverman's office and stared at me with her head vigilantly erect in case I might be a partridge.

"Shouldn't she be lying on the couch?" I said.

"She's not in analysis," Susan said.

"She belonged to your ex-husband."

"Yes," Susan said. "Good point."

The dog's eyes shifted from Susan to me as we spoke. The eyes were hazel and, because she was nervous, they showed a lot of white. Her short brown coat was sleek, like a seal's, and her oversized paws looked exaggerated, like a cartoon dog.

"What's her name?" I said.

Susan wrinkled her nose. *"Vigilant Virgin."*

"And she's not in analysis?"

"I believe they have to have long silly names like that because of the American Kennel Club," Susan said. "She's a hunting dog."

"I know," I said. "I had one like her when I was a kid."

"Like her?"

"Yeah. Same breed, same color, which is not usual. Mine was bigger though."

"Don't listen," Susan said to the dog. "You're perfectly big enough."

The dog canted her head at Susan, and raised her ears slightly.

"What are we going to do with her?" Susan said.

"We? My ex-husband didn't give her to me," I said.

"Well, he gave her to me, and what's mine is yours."

"Not if I have to walk around calling her *Vigilant Virgin,*" I said.

"What was your dog's name?" Susan said.

"Pearl."

"Well, let's call her Pearl."

"And Boink Brain isn't going to want her back?" I said.

"He's not so bad," Susan said.

"Anyone who let you get away is a boink brain," I said.

"Well," Susan said, "perhaps you're right . . . anyway. He's been transferred to London, and you can't even bring a dog in there without a six-month quarantine."

"So she's yours for good," I said.

"Ours."

I nodded. The dog got off the couch quite suddenly, and walked briskly over and put her head on my lap and stood motionless, with her eyes rolled slightly upward looking at me obliquely.

I nodded. "Pearl," I said.

Susan smiled. "Beautiful Jewish-American girls don't grow up with hunting dogs," she said. "If they have dogs at all they are very small dogs with a little bow."

"Sure thing, little lady. This looks to me like man's work."

"I think so," Susan said.

I patted Pearl's head.

"You could have told him no," I said.

"He had nowhere else to place her," Susan said. "And she's a lovely dog."

Pearl sighed. It seemed a sigh of contentment though dogs are often mysterious and sometimes do things I don't understand. Which is true also of people.

"Do we have joint custody?" I said. "I get her on weekends?"

"I think she can stay here," Susan said. "I have a yard. But certainly she could come to your place for sleepovers."

"Bring her jammies and her records? We could make brownies?"

"Something like that," Susan said. "Of course this is the city. We can't let her run loose."

"Which means you'll need to fence your yard."

"I think it's the best thing for us to do," Susan said. "Don't you?"

"No question," I said. "We'll have to work our ass off, of course."

"Beautiful Jewish-American girls do not 'work their ass off,' they bring ice tea in a pretty pitcher to the large goy they've charmed into doing it."

"When do we get to that?"

"The charm?"

"Yeah."

"Well, you remember once you suggested something and I said I'd never done it because I was too embarrassed."

"Certainly. It's one of the two or three times you've ever blushed."

11

Susan smiled and nodded.

"Today?" I said.

She smiled more widely and nodded again. If a serpent had come by with an apple at that moment she'd have eaten it.

"Spenser's my name," I said. "Fences are my game."

"Do you require a charm down payment?" Susan said.

"Well," I said, "some small gesture of earnest intent might be appropriate."

"Not in front of the baby," Susan said.

Pearl was on the couch again, perfectly still, gazing at us as if she were smarter than we were, but patient.

"Of course not," I said. "What kind of fence would you like?"

"Let's go look at some, she can ride along with us and wait in the car."

"What could be better?" I said.

"You'll find out," Susan said and smiled that smile.

CHAPTER

2

Susan had selected a picket fence made of spaced 1-inch dowels in a staggered pattern. I was listening to the ball game and drilling holes in the stringers to accommodate the dowels when a voice said,

"Hi, Ozzie. Where's Harriet."

It was Paul Giacomin, wearing jeans and high-top sneakers and a black tee shirt that said on it *American Dance Festival, 1989,* in white letters. I had taken him in hand when he was a fifteen-year-old kid caught in his parents' divorce feud with no interests but television and no prospects but more of the same. He was twenty-five now, an inch taller than I was, and almost as graceful.

"Making iced tea in a pretty pitcher," I said. "What are you doing here?"

"I tried your apartment first, and then followed my instincts."

"Trained by a master," I said.

Paul came over and shook my hand and patted me on the shoulder. Susan came out of the house and told him how glad she was to see him and gave him a hug and kissed him. Her range of demonstrable emotion is maybe a little wider than mine.

"Wait until you see what we have," Susan said.

She was wearing a glossy black leotard-esque exercise outfit and white sneakers and a bright blue headband and she looked a lot like Hedy Lamarr would have looked if Hedy worked out. She ran back to the house and opened the back door and Pearl came surging out, jumped the three steps off the back porch and, with her ears back, and her mouth open, dashed around the backyard in a slowly imploding circle until she finally ran into me, bounced off, and jammed her head into Paul's groin.

"Jesus Christ," Paul said. Pearl jumped up with her forepaws on his chest, dropped back down, turned in a tight circle as if she were chasing her tail, and jumped up again trying to lap Paul's face before she dropped back down and streaked around the yard again. As she came by the second time, Susan got a hold on her collar and managed to force her to a barely contained stop.

"She gets over her shyness," Paul said, "she might be cute."

"Regal," I said.

"Regal."

"This is Pearl," Susan said. "I inherited her from my ex-husband because he's transferred to London, and her daddy is building her a fence."

"This is embarrassing," Paul said.

"Let's go get a beer," I said, "and you can see how regal she is inside."

It took Pearl maybe fifteen minutes to calm down, climb up into the white satin armchair in Susan's living room, turn around three times, and lie with her head on her back legs in a tight ball and watch us drink beer.

"I recall," Paul said to Susan, "that you used to kick me

14

"It's got that look, you know, that says it's empty."

"You have a key?" I said.

"No. I think she didn't want me walking in on her when she had a date. She was always a little embarrassed with me about dating."

"Want me to take a look?"

"Yes."

"Want to go with me?"

"Yes. I want more than that. I want you and me to find her."

"She's probably just off on a little trip with somebody," I said.

"Probably," he said, and I knew he didn't mean it.

"Your father?" Susan said.

Paul shook his head. "I haven't heard from him in maybe six years. I haven't a clue where he is. Once the tuition money stopped . . ." Paul shrugged.

"Okay," I said. "We'll find her."

"I have to know she's all right," Paul said.

"Sure," I said.

"Funny," Paul said. "Ten years ago you found me for her."

The dog uncurled from the chair and hopped down and stretched and came over and got up beside me where I was sitting on the couch and began to lick my face industriously. Her tongue was rough, which was probably useful for stripping meat from bones in the Pleistocene era, but served in the late 20th century as a kind of sloppy dermabrasion.

"It'll be even easier this time," I said with my face clenched. "We'll have a trained hunter to help us."

3

Paul had gone off to the American Rep Theater to watch a performance artist smear herself with chocolate. Susan and I, feeling a little middle class and uptown, went for drinks to the Ritz bar. It had begun to rain when we got there and I got several raindrop spots on my maroon silk tie while I stashed the car with the doorman. Even with the raindrops, I looked Ritz-worthy with my black cashmere blazer and my gray slacks. I had wanted to complete the look by wearing the cowboy boots that had been handmade for me in L.A. by Willie the Cobbler. But Susan reminded me that I tended to fall off them if I had more than one drink, so I settled for black cordovan loafers.

As we cut through the lobby toward the bar, Callahan, the houseman, nodded at me pleasantly. I shot him with my forefinger and he looked at Susan and whistled silently.

"The house dick just whistled at you," I said.

"At the Ritz?" Susan said.

"Shocking but true," I said.

"Which one is he?" Susan said.

"Big guy with a red nose and gray hair. Looks fatter than he is."

"He looks very discerning," Susan said.

We got a table by the window in the bar, where we could look out through the rain at the Public Gardens. Susan ordered a champagne cocktail. I had scotch and soda.

"No beer?" Susan said.

"Celebration," I said. "I'm here with you and Paul's home. Makes me feel celebratory."

"When did scotch become the drink of celebration?" Susan leaned her chin on her folded hands and rested her gaze on me. The experience was, as it always was, tangible. The weight of her serious intelligence in counterpoint to her playful spoiled princess was culminative.

"Sometimes it's champagne," I said. "Sometimes it's scotch."

The bar was dark. The rain slid down the big window, and the early evening light filtering through it was silvery and slight. Susan picked a cashew from the small bowl of mixed nuts on the table, and bit off maybe a third of it and chewed it carefully.

"I was seventeen," I said, "the first time I had anything but beer. We were bird hunting in Maine, my father and I, and a pointer, Pearl the first. We were looking for pheasant in an old apple orchard that hadn't been farmed in maybe fifty years. You had to go through bad cover to reach it, brambles, and small alder that was clumped together and tangled. My father was maybe thirty yards off to the right, and the dog was ahead, ranging, the way they do, and coming back with her tongue out and her tail erect, and looking at me, and then swinging back out in another arc."

"Did you train her to do that?" Susan said.

"No," I said. "It's in the genes, I guess. They'll range like that and come back; and they'll point birds instinctively, but you've got to teach them to hold the point. Otherwise they'll stalk in on the bird and flush it too soon, and it'll fly when you're out of range. Or, if they're really good, they'll kill the bird."

Susan ate another third of her cashew, and sipped some champagne cocktail. The light through the rain was getting grayer. The silver edge was thinning as the evening came down on us.

"All of a sudden I heard her bark—half hysterical bark, half growl—and she came loping back, stopping every few yards and turning and making her barking snarling sound that had some fear in it, and then she reached me and leaned in hard on my leg and stood like they do, with her front legs stiff and her tail down and her ears sort of flattened back, and growled. And the hair was stiff along her spine. And I remember thinking, 'Jesus, this must be the pheasant that ate Chicago.' We had just come out of the cover and into the orchard and I looked and there was a bear."

"A grizzly?" Susan said. Her eyes were fixed on me and they seemed bottomless and captivated, like a kid listening to ghost stories.

"No, they don't have grizzly bears in Maine. It was a black bear, he'd been feeding on the fallen apples that some of the trees were still producing. They must have been close to rotten, and they must have been fermenting in his stomach, because he was drunk."

"Drunk?"

"Yeah, bears do that sometimes. Usually it happens close to a town, because that's where there are apple orchards, and the forest ranger types dart them and haul them off to some other place in the woods to sober up. But no one had tranquilized this one. He was loose, upright, drunk, and swaying a little. I don't know how big he was. Maybe a hundred and fifty pounds or so. Maybe more. They can get bigger. Standing on his hind legs he looked a lot bigger than I was."

"What did you do?"

"Well, the dog was going crazy now, growling and making a kind of high whining noise, and the bear was reared up and grunting. They sound more like pigs than anything else. I had a shotgun full of birdshot, sevens, I think, and it might have annoyed the bear. It sure as hell wouldn't have stopped him. But I didn't have anything else and I was pretty sure if I ran it would chase me, and they can run about forty miles an hour, so it was going to catch me. So I just stood there with the shotgun leveled. It was a pump. I had one round in the chamber and three more in the magazine, and I prayed that if he charged and if I got him in the face it would make him turn. The dog was in a frenzy, dashing out a few feet and barking and snarling and then running back to lean against my leg. The bear reared up, swaying, and I can still remember how rank the bear smelled and the way everything moved so slowly. And then my father was beside me. He didn't make any noise coming. Afterwards he said he heard the dog and knew it was something, probably a bear, from the way the dog sounded. He had a shotgun too, but he also was carrying a big old .45 hogleg, a six-shooter he'd had ever since he was a kid in Laramie. And he stood beside the dog, next to me, and took that shooter's stance that I always can remember him using, and cocked the .45 and we waited. The bear dropped to all fours, and snorted and grunted and dipped its head and turned around and left. I can see us like a painting on a calendar, my father with the .45 and the dog between us, snarling, and yipping, and me with the shotgun that, if he'd charged, the bear would have picked his teeth with."

It was dark now outside the Ritz bar, and the rain coiling down the windowpane looked black. Susan had finished her cashew and was leaning back in her chair, holding her drink in both hands, watching me.

"The dog was no good for birds the rest of the day, and neither were we, I suppose. We went back to the lodge we were staying at and put Pearl in our room, and fed her, and then my father and I went down to the bar and my father ordered two double scotch whiskies. The bartender looked at me and looked at my father and didn't say anything and brought the whiskey. He put both of them in front of my father and my father pushed one of them over in front of me.

" 'Ran into a bear in the woods today,' my father said without much inflection. He still had the Western sound in his voice. 'Kid stood his ground.'

"The bartender was a lean, dark guy, with a big nose. He looked at me and nodded and moved on down the bar, and my father and I drank the scotch."

"And he never said anything to you," Susan said.

I shook my head.

" 'That brown liquor,' " Susan said, " 'which not women, not boys and children, but only hunters drank.' "

"Faulkner," I said.

Susan smiled. "You're very literate for a man who has to buy extra-long ties."

"I had acted like a man, in his view, so he treated me like a man, in his view."

22

" 'Not women, not boys and children,' " Susan said.

"Sounds ageist and sexist to me," I said.

"Maybe we can have his Nobel prize posthumously revoked," Susan said.

4

Paul and I were driving out Route 2 toward Lexington to break into Paul's mother's house. It was the first day that had felt like fall this year. And it was still raining, a lighter rain than last night, but steady so that the streets glistened and the cars had their lights on even though it was well after sunrise.

Pearl was sitting in the backseat looking steadily out the window on the passenger side, mostly motionless except when she turned her head to look out the other window. She had wanted very much to come and neither Paul nor I could quite think of a reason sufficient to leave her staring after us with that look.

A school bus passed us going the other way and I felt the pang I always felt in early fall, the remembered pang of school. So many days like this I remembered in the brick elementary school, the lights on inside, the day wet and shiny outside, cars moving past the school with their wipers going, and the smell of steam pipes and disinfectant and limitation and tedium, while outside the adult world moved freely about.

"How was it last night?" I said. I was drinking a cup of

coffee as I drove, something I prided myself on doing with the cover off and never a drop spilled. Paul drank his out of a hole he'd torn in the cover. A boy still, with things to learn.

"She's good," Paul said, "very interesting. Essentially it's just a one-woman show, like, ah, whosis, Lily Tomlin, except a lot more angry and foulmouthed."

"I never heard of her," I said.

"I know her from New York," Paul said. "She's just a regular downtown performer, like me, trying to find performance space someplace in the East Village, except that she was lucky enough to be denied an NEA grant. Now she's making big money. And playing high-visibility theaters. And getting written up in *Time.*"

"Have you thought of applying?"

"The tricky part is to make a grant application good enough to get approved by the peer review panel, and still exotic enough to be officially rejected."

"Maybe I should take Susan," I said.

Paul laughed. "She might like it," he said. "You'd hate it."

We pulled off into Lexington. The traffic was at a crawl, stuck behind a school bus that stopped every few blocks and took on children.

"Do you know your mother's new boyfriend?" I said.

Paul shook his head. "Never met him. His name is Rich something or other."

"What's he do?"

"My mother says he's a consultant."

"Self-employed?"

Paul shook his head. "I don't know. She seemed a little vague about what he did. She never wants to talk much about any of her boyfriends. Like I said, she's always embarrassed about them."

We went through the middle of Lexington, past the Battle Green, with the Minuteman statue at the near end of it and the restored colonial buildings across the street. Paul was staring around at the town as if it were a Martian landscape.

"Every Patriots Day there was a big parade in town," Paul said. "It was always exciting. Every April 19, I'd wake up excited, and my mother and father and I would come down and get a good spot and watch for the parade, and afterwards we'd go home and there'd be nothing to do and I'd feel let down, and the next day would be school."

I turned into Emerson Road.

"Parade was usually good, though," Paul said.

Patty Giacomin's house was as I remembered it, set back a bit from the road, among trees. The trees were probably fuller than they had been ten years ago when I'd come out here before. But they looked the same and so did the dense spread of pachysandra that did service as lawn around her house.

The house itself was angular, and shingled; modern looking without violating either the site or the colonial town in which it stood.

I parked next to a Honda Prelude in the driveway. We rolled the windows half down and left Pearl in the car. I went and opened the trunk and took out a gym bag with tools in it. As we walked toward the house I automatically felt the hood of the Prelude. It was cold.

There was no answer when we rang the bell. The house had that stillness that Paul had mentioned. In the interests of not looking like a jerk, I tried the doorknob. It was locked.

"I already did that," Paul said.

"It's a Dick Tracy crime stopper," I said. "Always try the door before jimmying it."

"Great working with a pro," Paul said.

There was no sign of flies on the inside of the windows, which was encouraging. I looked at the door. There was a keyhole in the handle. No other lock, so it was probably a spring lock, though it didn't have to be. It could be a combination spring and deadbolt, but at least there was no separate keyhole which would be most certainly for a deadbolt. There was a strip of molding down along the lock side of the door to prevent someone from slipping a flat blade like a putty knife in there and springing the lock. I looked at the molding closely. The house was stained rather than painted, which made it easier to see the line where the molding butted up to the doorjamb. While I was examining it, I took a deep inhale. I smelled nothing dead, which was even more encouraging.

"Okay," I said. "I'll open this thing unless you have a better thought."

Paul shook his head. His face looked tight. I took a flat chisel from the bag, and a hammer, and gently loosened the molding along the door strip. No point trashing the house.

"I'll get this off intact," I said. "We can put it back on when we get through."

Paul nodded. I pried the molding away, a little at a time, all along its length, and then got a flat bar under it at the nail holes and pried it carefully loose so that it came off nails still sticking through it. I handed it to Paul and he leaned it against a tree. I put the flat bar and the chisel and the hammer away and got out a putty knife with an inch and a half blade and slid it into the door crack at the latch

27

and felt for the lock tongue. I found it and pressed and felt the tongue give and the blade of the putty knife push in. I held the putty knife in place with my right hand, and with the flat of my left, pushed the door open. There was no smell.

"We're not going to find anything bad," I said to Paul. "Promise."

"That's good," he said. His voice was a little hoarse.

We were in a small entry hall, with a polished flagstone floor, then up a couple of steps to the living room, the kitchen to the right, a view of the woods straight ahead through the big picture window across the back. Off the kitchen, constituting a short L to the living room, was a dining area where once Patty Giacomin had served me dinner and propositioned me. It hadn't been me, really, just the need to validate herself with a man, and there I was. I had declined, but I remembered it well. I always thought about the ones I'd missed, and speculated about how they'd have been, even though wisdom and experience would suggest that they'd have been much like the ones I hadn't missed. The thing was, though, that I always thought about the ones I hadn't missed, too.

The house was still and close, and neat. We walked around, checked the bedrooms. Patty's big, pink, puffy bed was made, her bathroom was orderly, though it didn't look like it had been put in order by someone who was leaving. Around the mirror were postcards with amusing pictures.

"I sent her those," Paul said, "from wherever I was performing. She kept them."

The other bedroom, where Paul had slept, was perfectly neat, with a high school picture of Paul still in its cardboard frame set up on the dresser. The picture had been taken the year he'd graduated from prep school, three years after I'd met him, and already the aimlessness had disappeared from his face. He was still very young there, but it was a face that knew more than most eighteen-year-old faces knew.

Paul looked at the picture. "Three years of therapy," he said.

"And more to come," I said.

"For sure," he said.

There was a neat green corduroy spread over the single bed, with a plaid blanket folded neatly at the foot. There was a student desk with a reading lamp on it and a green blotter that matched the spread.

We went back downstairs. On the coffee table in the living room was a green imitation leather scrapbook. I picked it up and opened it. Carefully pasted in were clippings: reviews of Paul's dance concerts, listings from the newspaper of performances to come. There were ticket stubs and program covers and the program pages listing Paul's name, or Paige's or both. There were pictures of Paul, often with Paige, sometimes with other dancers, taken in places domestic and foreign, where they had danced. I handed the album to him without comment and he took it and looked at it and sat down slowly on the couch and leafed slowly through it.

"I used to think," he said, "that because she was so needy of my father, and after she lost him, so needy for other men, that she didn't care about me." He turned the pages in the album slowly, as he talked. He'd seen them already. He wasn't looking at them. It was merely something the hands did. "Sort of an *either-or* situation. *Me* or

29

them. It took me a long time to see that it was both. That she cared about me, too."

"As best she could," I said.

"Her best wasn't enough," Paul said.

"No. It's why we separated you."

"And we were right," Paul said.

"Yeah."

Paul closed the album and put it back on the coffee table.

"If she'd gotten some help, maybe if she would have seen somebody . . ."

I shrugged.

"You don't think so."

"No," I said. "I don't think she's smart enough. I don't think she's got enough will."

Paul nodded slowly. He looked down at the scrapbook on the coffee table.

"She is what she is," he said.

5

Paul went out to the car and brought Pearl in. She raced around the house with her nose to the ground for about fifteen minutes before she was able to slow down and follow me around while I searched the house.

The refrigerator was on, but nearly empty, and there was nothing perishable in it. There was no fruit in the bowl on the table. The strainer was out of the drain in the kitchen sink. There was no suitcase to be found in the house, which meant either that she had packed it and taken it with her or that she didn't have one. Paul didn't know if she had one, and he couldn't tell if any of her clothes were missing. There were very few cosmetics in the bathroom. There were eleven messages on her answering machine, three from Paul. I copied down the names and phone numbers that had been left. Mostly they were first names only, and Paul didn't know who they were. But the phone numbers could lead to something. I couldn't find an address book.

"Did she have one?" I said.

"Yes. I know she did. She carried it around with her and she was always afraid of losing it."

"She work?"

"Yes. She sold real estate. Worked for a company called *Chez Vous.*"

"Cute."

"Hey," Paul said. "We're in the suburbs. *Cute* is important out here."

"You New York kids are so jaded," I said. "Do you know where she met Rich?"

"No."

"Probably a dating bar called *Entre Nous,*" I said.

"Or *Cherchez la Femme,*" Paul said.

"That betrays a preconception about dating bars," I said.

"I suppose it does," Paul said. "How about what you've found here? You have any conclusions to reach?"

"Everything here says that she left of her own accord," I said. "There's no mail piled up, which means she stopped it at the post office. There's no suitcase. Most people have one, which suggests that she took it. There's a dearth of cosmetics, which suggests that she packed them. The house is neat, but not like no one's ever coming back. There are no perishables in the refrigerator, which suggests that she was planning to be gone for a while."

"Without telling me?"

"We agree that's she's not Mother Courage," I said.

"True."

"You want me to find where she went?"

"I feel like kind of a jerk," Paul said. "I wouldn't want the police involved."

"But you'd still like to know where she is," I said.

Paul nodded. "I think she'd have called, or written me a postcard, something."

glasses sat at one of the remaining desks speaking on the phone. She was speaking about a house that the office was listing and she was being enthusiastic. The other desk was occupied by a very slender blonde woman wearing a lot of clothes. Her white skirt reached her ankles, nearly covering her black-laced high-heeled boots. Over the skirt she wore a longish ivory-colored tunic and a black leather belt with a huge buckle and a small crocheted beige sleeveless sweater, and a beige scarf at her neck, and ivory earrings that were carved in the shape of Japanese dolls, and rings on all her fingers, and a white bow in her hair.

"Hi, I'm Nancy," she said. "Can I help?"

I took a card out of my shirt pocket and gave it to her. It had my name on it, and my address and phone number and the word Investigator. Nothing else. Susan had said that a Tommy gun, with a fifty-round drum, spewing flame from the muzzle, was undignified.

"I'm representing Paul Giacomin, whose mother works here."

Nancy was still eyeballing the card. "Does this mean, like a *Private* Investigator?"

I smiled winningly and nodded.

"Like a Private Eye?"

"The stuff that dreams are made of, sweetheart," I said.

The woman with the blue-black hair hung up the phone.

"Hey, PJ," Nancy said. "This is a Private Eye."

"Like on television?" PJ said. Where Nancy was flat, PJ was curved. Where Nancy was overdressed, PJ wore a sleeveless crimson blouse and gray slacks which fitted very smoothly over her sumptuous thighs. She had bare ankles and high-heeled red shoes. Around her left ankle was a gold chain.

"Just like television," I said. "Car chases, shoot-outs, beautiful broads . . ."

"Which is where we come in," PJ said. She had on pale lipstick and small gold earrings. There were small laugh wrinkles around her eyes, and she looked altogether like more fun than was probably legal in Lexington.

"My point exactly," I said. "I'm trying to locate Patty Giacomin."

"For her son?" Nancy said.

"Yes. She's apparently gone, and he doesn't know where and he wants to."

"I don't blame him," PJ said.

"You know where she is?"

Both women shook their heads. "She hasn't been in for about ten days," PJ said.

"A week ago last Monday," Nancy said.

"Is that usual?"

"No. I mean, it's not like she's on salary. She doesn't come in, she doesn't get listings, she doesn't sell anything, she doesn't get commission," PJ said. "But usually she was in here three, four days a week—she was sort of part-time."

"Who runs the place?"

"I do," PJ said.

"Are you *Chez* or *Vous?*"

PJ grinned. "Is that awful, or what? No. My name's P. J. Garfield. PJ stands for Patty Jean. But with Patty Giacomin working here, it was easier to use PJ, saved confusion. I bought the place from the previous owner when she retired. *Chez Vous* was her idea. I didn't want to change the name."

"Either of you know Patty's boyfriend?" I said.

"Rich?" Nancy said.

"Rich what?"

Nancy looked at PJ. She shrugged.

"Rich . . ." PJ said. "Rich . . . she brought him to the Christmas party last year. An absolute hunk. Rich . . . Broderick, I think, something like that. Rich Broderick? Bachrach? Beaumont?"

"Beaumont," Nancy said.

"You sure?"

"Oh." She put her hand to her mouth. "No, god no, I'm not sure. I don't want anyone to get in trouble."

"How nice," I said. "Do we know where Rich lives?"

"Somewhere on the water," Nancy said. She looked at PJ.

PJ shrugged. "Could be. I frankly paid very little attention to him. He's not Patty's first boyfriend. And most of them are not, ah, *mensches.*"

"What can you remember?" I said.

"Me?" Nancy said.

"Either of you. What did he look like? What did he do for a living? What did he talk about? Did he like baseball, or horse racing, or sailboats? Was he married, separated, single, divorced? Did he have children? Did he have any physical handicap, any odd mannerisms, did he have an accent? Did he mention parents, brothers, sisters? Did he like dogs?"

PJ answered. "He was as tall as you, probably not as"—she searched for the word—"thick. Dark hair worn longish, good haircut"—her eyes crinkled—"great buns."

"So we have that in common too," I said. Nancy looked at her desk.

37

"His clothes were expensive," PJ said. "And they fit him well. He's probably a good off-the-rack size."

"What size?"

"What size are you?" PJ said.

"Fifty," I said, "fifty-two, depends."

"He'd probably be a forty-four, maybe. He's more, ah, willowy."

"How grand for him," I said.

"I like husky men, myself," PJ said.

"Phew!"

"He didn't have an accent," Nancy said.

"You mean he talked like everyone else around here?"

"No. I mean he had no accent at all," Nancy said. "Like a radio announcer. He didn't sound like he was from here. He didn't sound like he was from the South, or from anywhere."

Nancy was maybe a little keener than she seemed.

"Good-looking guy?" I said.

Nancy nodded very vigorously. PJ noticed it and grinned.

"He was pretty as hell," she said. "Straight nose, dimple in his chin, kind of pouty lips, smooth-shaven, though you could see that his beard is dark. Kind of man that wears cologne, silk shorts."

Nancy got a little touch of pink on her cheekbones.

"Okay," I said. "The consensus is that his name is Rich Beaumont, or thereabouts, that he's six feet one, maybe a hundred eighty-five pounds, dark longish hair, well styled, good clothes, handsome, and particularly attractive to slender blonde women."

"What do you mean?" Nancy said.

"A wild guess," I said. "He speaks in an accentless way, and lives near the water."

38

"Hell," PJ said. "We knew more than we thought we did."

"Masterful questioning," I said, "brings it out. You have any thoughts at all about where Patty Giacomin might be?"

"No. Really," Nancy said, "I can't imagine."

"You find the boyfriend," PJ said, "you'll probably find her. Patty doesn't do much without a man. Usually not that good a man."

"Thank you," I said. "The kid's worried. If you hear anything, please call me."

"Certainly," Nancy said.

PJ grinned so that her eyes crinkled a little.

"You had lunch?" she said.

"Can't," I said. "I got a dog in the car."

"An actual dog or is that an unkind euphemism?"

"An actual dog, named Pearl. Can euphemisms be unkind?"

"I don't know. There's always dinner? Or are you married?"

"Well, I have a friend."

"Don't they all," PJ said. "Too bad. We'd have had fun."

"Yeah," I said. "We would have in fact."

I went out of *Chez Vous,* and went back to the car.

7

When I got to my car, Pearl was curled tightly in the driver's seat. She sprang up when I opened the door and insinuated herself between the bucket front seats into the back. When I got in she lapped the side of my face vigorously.

"I thought you were Susan's dog," I said.

She made no response.

Back in my office she guzzled down some water from a bowl placed for that purpose by Paul.

"Did you know that they drink by curling their tongue backwards?" I said. "Under?"

"How exciting," Paul said. "Thank you for sharing that with me."

"How'd you do on the phone?"

"Not very well," he said. "No one knew where she was. Some of the calls were from real estate customers who don't know anything about her. One woman said she was my mother's best friend. I figure she's worth a visit."

"She know anything?"

"She was late for aerobics, she said. But I could call later."

"Better to visit," I said. "Where is she?"

"Lives in Concord. She gave me the address."

"Okay. I'll run out and have a talk with her," I said.

"I'll go with you."

"No need to."

"Yes," Paul said. "There is a need to."

"Okay."

"You took care of everything when I was fifteen," he said. "I'm not fifteen now. I need to do part of this."

"Sure," I said. Paul's presence would make it harder. People would be less frank about Patty in front of her son. But he wasn't fifteen anymore and it was his mother. Pearl had gotten herself up onto the narrow client's chair and was curled precariously, mouthing the yellow tennis ball she'd tracked down on a walk in Cambridge. Her eyes followed every movement I made. I got her leash and snapped it on and took her to the car and drove her and Paul to Concord.

Most of the way up Route 2 she had her head on my left shoulder, her nose out the open window, sampling the wind.

"It is not entirely clear," I said to Paul, "why I am bringing this hound with me everywhere I go."

"Cathexis," Paul said.

"I knew you'd know."

"What did they say about my mother?" he said.

"The people at *Chez Vous?*"

"*Oui.*"

"They had no real idea where she might be."

"I know, you told me that. But what did they say?"

"They said she worked, usually, three or four days a week, on commission. That she had brought Rich to a

41

Christmas party last year and that he was very good looking."

"That all?"

"They didn't exactly say, but made it quite clear that
they thought that your mother's choices of men were
often ill-advised."

"Many men?"

"They suggested that she needed to be with a man, and
that if we found Rich we'd find her."

"Did they talk about her need to be with men?"

"Not a lot. They seemed to record it as a fact of your
mother's nature that she wasn't likely to go very far, very
often, without the company of a man."

"That could get you in trouble," Paul said.

I nodded. We left Route 2, onto 2A, which was the old
Revolutionary War road, where the embattled farmers
sniped at the redcoats from behind the fieldstone walls.
We passed historic houses—the Wayside, the Alcott
House—all the way into Concord center.

Not all of the historical places in Massachusetts look the
way you'd like them to. But Concord does. It has over-
arching trees, spacious colonial homes, a green, a clean
little downtown made mostly of red brick, a rambling
white clapboard inn that looks as if stagecoaches should
still be stopping there. There are the historic sights, the
academy, the river where one can rent a canoe and spend
a day of transcendental paddling, as Susan and I had occasionally done, pausing to picnic one day almost beneath
the rude bridge that arched the flood.

The address we wanted was a recycled jelly factory in
downtown Concord. They'd sandblasted the brick and
cleaned up the clock tower and gutted the interior and

built blond-wood-with-white-walls condominium apartments inside. Out back was a big parking lot. A hopeful sales office was still open on the first floor of the building.

The woman's name was Caitlin Moore. She answered the bell in a pink spandex leotard, white sneakers, and a pink sweatband. She was built like the cheerleaders of my youth, chunky, bouncy, not very tall. Her extremely blonde hair was caught into a ponytail. She had on green eye shadow and false eyelashes and whitish lip gloss, which made her look a little spectral.

"Hi," she said, friendly. "I'm Caitlin. You must be Paul, who I talked with on the phone."

Paul said he was, and introduced me.

"You're a detective?"

"Yes."

"Could I see something?"

"Sure." I gave her my license, she looked at it for a moment, then went to a bleached oak table and got a pair of half-glasses and put them on and came back looking further at my license. "Well," she said. "A hard man is good to find."

She smiled. I smiled. Paul smiled.

"Come on in," Caitlin said. "Want some coffee? All I got is instant, but I can microwave it in no time."

Paul and I declined. Caitlin led us into her sitting room, her prominent little butt waggling ahead of us as we followed her. With its bleached woodwork and stark white walls and ceiling, and anodized combination windows, the room was standard condo modern. It appeared to have been furnished by Betsy Ross. There was an old maple standup desk, an antique pine harvest table, a pine thumbback rocker, a coffee table made from a cobbler's

43

bench. It went with the room the way Liberace goes with
Faust.

"I love early American," she said as we sat down. Paul
and me on the sofa. Caitlin on the thumbback rocker,
where she crossed both legs under her. "When I got divorced I made the bastard give me all the furniture."

"Great," I said.

"You're my mother's best friend?" Paul said.

"Oh, absolutely," Caitlin said. "Patty and I are like
twins. She's always talking about you."

"What does she say?"

"She talks about how successful you are. You're in the
movies, I think?"

"I'm a dancer in New York," Paul said. "I was on screen
for a minute and twenty-six seconds in a film about American Dance that played on PBS."

"Yuh, I knew it was something like that. Anyway, we
been really close ever since we were in aerobics together
at Sweats Plus. Something about us, you know, we just hit
it off. Both been divorced and all. I don't have any kids,
but, well, we knew something about pain, and recovery."

"Know her current boyfriend?" I said.

"I introduced them."

"Tell us a little about him," Paul said.

"He's a real doll. Friend of my brother's. I knew Patty
was looking to go out, and I knew Rich was single. So
I . . ." Caitlin spread her hands and shrugged. "They really
connected, you know, right from the start. It was something. You worried about her? Maybe she and Rich just
went off, they were crazy like that, I don't mean anything
bad about your mom, Paul, she was just ready for fun
anytime. I bet they just went off somewhere for a while
on the spur."

"They have a place they usually go?" I said.

"Oh, they'd go anywhere. I don't know. Miami, Atlantic City, Club Med. You name it."

"What's Rich's last name?" Paul said.

"Beaumont. Rich Beaumont." She pronounced it with the stress on the last syllable.

"Where's he live?" I said.

"Over in Revere someplace, I think. On the water. I think he's got a condo on the beach."

"Got an address?"

"No, not really. I don't think I ever knew it exactly."

"Phone number?"

Caitlin smiled and spread her hands. "I'd always meet him through my brother."

"Can we talk with your brother?" Paul said.

"Marty? I don't know what Marty can tell you."

"How's your brother know Rich?"

"I don't know, they play handball together. Double date. I think they did some business sometime."

"What's Rich's business?"

"Consultant."

"You know what he consults in?"

"No, just some kind of consulting business."

"What's your brother do?"

"Marty's a paving contractor. Hot top, you know, that stuff."

"And his last name?" I said.

"Martinelli."

"Martin Martinelli?" I said.

"Yeah. My mother was a lunatic. How about Caitlin Martinelli? My old lady was nuts."

"What was it like being my mother's friend?" Paul said.

"Huh?"

"What's she like?"

"You're her kid," Caitlin said. "You should know—better than anybody."

"I should but I don't. What does she care about?"

The question was too hard for Caitlin. She frowned. "What did she care about?"

"Yeah."

Caitlin lifted her shoulders. "Ah . . ." Caitlin waved her hands vaguely. "She, ah. She liked aerobics. You know she cared about her body, and how she looked. And she knew a lot about makeup."

Paul nodded.

Caitlin had a thread to follow out of her confusion. She tumbled on. "And fun," Caitlin said. "Patty loved to have fun."

Paul nodded again.

"Who were her other close friends?" I said.

"I don't really know her other friends. . . . She had a friend named Sonny, was a traffic reporter, you know, from a helicopter."

"Man or woman?" I said.

"Woman."

"She have a last name?"

"Oh, sure. I mean, doesn't everybody? I don't know it, though. Just Sonny."

"Know the station she reported for?"

Caitlin shook her head.

"We'd like to talk with your brother," I said. "Could you give us an address?"

Caitlin looked flustered. "Gee, I don't know. Marty won't be too thrilled. Marty's a very private guy. Very successful businessman, very private."

"I know his name," I said. "I know his business. I can find him. Will he like me finding him, asking around about him?"

"God, no. Listen. I'll give you his work address. That way you won't be bothering him at home."

"Sure," I said.

She gave me an address on the Revere Beach Parkway in Everett.

"Did she ever talk about my father?" Paul said.

"Her ex-? What's-his-name, Mel? Sure did. She called him a cheap sonovabitch every chance she could. Excuse me, I know he's your dad and all."

"That's okay," Paul said. "I can hear whatever there is to hear. I *need* to hear it."

"Well, don't worry about her. I'm sure she's off someplace with Rich having a ball. Your mother is a fun lady!"

"You don't think she might go someplace without Rich?" Paul said.

Caitlin looked startled. "No," she said. "Of course not. What fun is it alone?"

47

8

Susan said, "When Pearl sleeps with you does she get under the covers?"

We were sitting at the same table in the Ritz bar. On a Wednesday with the baseball season dwindling, and the kids grimly back in school. It was raining again. The Ritz bar is a good place to spend a rainy weekday afternoon.

"Of course," I said. "Don't you?"

"I'm not sure all dogs do that," Susan said.

"We shouldn't generalize," I said.

Susan nodded. "True," she said.

I was drinking Sam Adams. Susan had a glass of riesling which would last her the day. The bar was nearly empty. It wasn't the old Ritz bar. It had been refurbished by new owners into something that looked like an English hunting club, or the last twenty-five hotel bars you'd been in. But you could still have a table by the window, looking out at Arlington Street and the Public Gardens.

"What do you think about Paul?" I said. "It's not just that he wants to locate his mother. He wants to find out about her."

"He's thinking about getting married," Susan said.

"Yeah?"

"For a kid like Paul whose parents' marriage was a failure, whose own life has made him careful, and introspective, the idea of marriage carries with it heavy baggage."

"His mother really is missing," I said.

"His mother has always been missing."

"Mine too," I said.

Susan took a gram of riesling and swallowed it carefully and put the glass back down. She looked out at the wet street for a moment.

"How long have we been together?" she said.

"If you date *together* from the time I first got your clothes off," I said, "sixteen years."

"Aren't you the romantic fool," Susan said.

"How do you date it?" I said.

Susan thought a minute. Outside, chic Back Bay women were picking their way past the rain puddles on their high heels, bending in under the little black umbrellas they all had, most of them holding skirts down by pressing their left hand and forearm across their thighs as the wind pushed at them.

"I'd say it begins with the time you first got my clothes off."

"September," I said. "Nineteen seventy-four. After Labor Day. It's almost an anniversary now that I think of it. You had on red undies with big black polka dots and a little black bow on the side."

"Selected with great care," Susan said. "I planned that you'd get my clothes off."

Outside on Arlington Street, the taxis all had their lights on in the rain and the overcast. The Yellow headlights

mixed with the neon and the traffic lights to make glisten-
ing streaks on the wet pavement—red, green, and yellow
mostly. Two young Boston cops strolled past, heading toward Park Square, their slickers gleaming in the rain, the
plastic covers on their hats looking oddly out of keeping.

"In all that time," Susan said, "you have spoken maybe
for five minutes, total, about your past."

"My past?"

"Yes, your past."

"What is this, an old Bette Davis movie?"

"No," Susan said. "I know you as I am sure no one in the
world knows you. But I only know you since we undressed
that first time in September 1974. I don't to this day know
how you got to be what you are. I don't know about other
women, about family, about what you were like as a little
boy, peeking out at the adult world, trying to grow up,
getting scarred in the process."

"Heavens," I said.

Susan smiled. Dampened the tip of her tongue with her
wine. I drank the rest of my Sam Adams. The waiter
noticed and raised an inquiring eyebrow. I nodded and he
hustled over a fresh bottle on a silver tray.

"It's a rainy day," Susan said. "We have nothing to do
but look at the rain and watch the people go by on whatever street that is out there."

"You've lived here since the Johnstown flood," I said.
"That's Arlington Street, runs from Beacon Street in the
north to Tremont Street in the South End."

Susan smiled the smile she always smiled when you
knew she hadn't the slightest interest in what you were
saying, and she knew it, and she knew you knew it.

"Of course," she said.

The only other people in the bar were two women at a table, with Bonwit's shopping bags piled on the two empty chairs; and a guy at the bar, reading *The Wall Street Journal* and sipping what looked like a Gibson, up. The women were drinking white wine. Both of them smoked. Susan settled her gaze on me and waited.

"Well, we had a dog named Pearl," I said.

"I know that," Susan said. "And I know that you were born in Laramie, Wyoming, and that your mother died while she carried you and you were born by cesarean section and your father and your two uncles, who were your mother's brothers, raised you."

"Me and Macbeth," I said.

"Not of woman born," Susan said. "But that's all I know."

"And all ye need to know," I said.

"Many people would welcome the chance to sit in a quiet bar on a rainy afternoon and talk about themselves to an attentive listener," Susan said. "Many people pay one hundred and fifty dollars an hour to come and sit in a quiet office and talk to me about themselves."

"Do they know you used to wear polka dot panties with a bow?" I said.

"Most of them don't."

I drank some beer. I looked out the window at the wet, wind-driven cityscape. *The small rain down can rain.*

"My father was a carpenter," I said, "in business with his wife's two brothers. They were very young when I was born. My uncles were seventeen and eighteen. My father was twenty."

"My God," Susan said. "Children raising children."

"I suppose so," I said. "But this was the depression,

51

remember, and people grew up early those years. Everyone worked as soon as he could, especially in a place like
Laramie."

"Your father never remarried."

"No."

"And your uncles lived with you?"

"Yeah, until they got married. They both married late.
I was in my teens."

"So you grew up in an all-male household."

I nodded.

"My uncles dated a lot, so did my father. There were
always girlfriends around. But they didn't have anything
to do with the family. The family was us."

"Three men and a boy," Susan said.

"Maybe four boys," I said.

"All unified by a connection to one woman."

"Yeah."

"Who was dead," Susan said.

I nodded.

"They were all fighters," I said. "My father used to pick
up spare money boxing, around the state, at smokers,
fairs, stuff like that. And my uncles did the same thing.
Heavyweight, all three of them. One uncle fought for a
while at light heavy until he filled out."

"And they taught you."

"Yeah. I could box as far back as I can remember."

"What were they like?" Susan said.

"They were like each other," I said. "Other than that
it's hard to summarize. They were fairly wild, tough men.
But one thing was clear. We were family, the four of us,
and in that family I was the treasure."

"They loved you."

"They loved me without reservation," I said. "No conditions. Nothing about their love depended on my grades or my behavior. They expected me to learn how to act by observing them. And God save anyone who didn't treat me properly."

"Like what?" Susan said. I could see how she'd gotten to be such a good shrink. Her interest was luminous. She listened with her whole self. Her eyes picked up every movement of my hands, every gesture of my soul.

"I went to the store once," I said, "and on the way back, past a saloon, a couple of drunks gave me a hard time. I was probably sort of mouthy."

"Hard to believe," Susan murmured.

"Anyway—I was maybe around ten—the bottle of milk I was carrying got broken. I went home and told my uncle Bob, who was the only one there. One of them was always home. I never had a babysitter. And he grinned and said we'd take care of it, and later that afternoon, we all went down to the place. It was called the Blind Pig Saloon, and my father and my uncles cleaned it out. It was like one of those old John Wayne movies, where bodies would come flying out through the front window. I didn't know if the culprits were even in there when we arrived. Didn't matter. By the time the cops came the place was empty except for me, and everything in there was broken."

"Where were you," Susan said, "while all this was happening?"

"Mostly behind the bar, watching, like the kid in *Shane.* Even had the dog with me."

We were quiet. Susan twirled the stem of her nearly full wineglass. There was the imprint of her lipstick on the rim. I thought about what it might be like going through life with everything having a faint raspberry flavor.

"Parents' day at school was an event," I said. "They'd

always come. The three of them. All six feet or more. All around two hundred pounds and hard as the handle on a pickax, and they'd sit in the back row, at the little desks, with their arms folded and not say a word. But they always came."

Across Arlington Street, past the wrought-iron fence that rimmed the Public Gardens, beyond the initial stand of big trees, I could see the weeping willows that stood around the lagoon where the swan boats drifted in pleasant weather. Through the rain the willows had a misty green blur about them, softened by the weather, almost lacy.

"When I was ten or twelve," I said, "we moved east. I think my father and my uncles thought it was a better place for a kid to grow up."

"Boston?" Susan said.

"Yeah. The Athens of America. My father read a lot. My uncles didn't, except to me. Every night one of them would read to me after dinner while the other two cleaned up."

"What did they read?"

"To me? Uncle Remus, Winnie-the-Pooh, Joseph Altscheler, John R. Tunis, stuff like that."

"And what did your father read, to himself?" Susan said.

"He had no formal education, so he had no master plan," I said. "He read whatever came along: Shakespeare, Kenneth Roberts, Faulkner, C. S. Forester, Dos Passos, Rex Stout. Actually I think he was reading Marquand when he decided to move us to Boston. Or Oliver Wendell Holmes, or Henry Adams, somebody like that."

"Because he thought it would be good for you?"

"Yeah. He believed all that Hub of the Universe stuff."

"So you all came."

"Oh yeah, the four of us and Pearl."

"And what about love? Was there someone before me?"

"There were a lot of women before you."

"No. I mean, did you ever love anyone before me?"

"Just once," I said.

"Was she as pretty, sexy, and smart as I am?" Susan said.

"Would you believe, prettier, sexier, and smarter."

"No," Susan said.

"How about younger?" I said.

"Younger is possible."

9

R & B Hot Top and Paving was behind a ragged shopping center off the Revere Beach Parkway in Everett. A red sign with yellow letters that appeared to have been hand painted on a piece of 4 × 8 plywood was nailed to a utility pole out front. There were a couple of asphalt-stained dump trucks parked on the hot-top turnaround, and, next to the Quonset hut that served as an office, a power roller was parked on a trailer. The hot-top apron was maybe four inches thick and gleamed the way new hot top does, but no one had bothered to retain it and it was crumbly and scattered along the edges.

In the backseat Pearl growled in an entirely uncute way, and the hair along her spine went up. A black and tan pit bull terrier appeared in the door of the Quonset with his head down and stared out at the car.

"Pearl appears to want a piece of that pit bull," Paul said.

"That's because she's in here," I said. Paul and I got out of the car carefully so Pearl would stay put. She was stiff-legged in the backseat, growling a low serious growl. The pit bull gazed at us, his yellow eyes unblinking.

"Nice doggie," Paul murmured.

"I'm not sure that's going to work," I said.

We walked toward the door. A squat man appeared in it wearing a gold tank top and blue workout pants with red trim. He had dark curly hair, worn longish, over his ears, and there was a lot of dark hair on his chest and arms. As we got close I could see that he was wearing a small gold loop in his left ear. There were two gold chains around his neck, a gold bracelet on his right wrist, a gold Rolex watch on his left one. On his feet he wore woven leather sandals.

The pit bull growled briefly. The man bent over slightly and took hold of the loose end of the dog's choke collar.

"He won't bother you unless I tell him," the man said.

"Good to know," I said.

"We're looking for Marty Martinelli," Paul said.

"What for?" the man said. The pit bull was motionless, his expressionless yellow eyes staring at us. There was a barely audible rumble in his throat. The man had a forefinger hooked less firmly than I would have liked through the ring on the choke collar. On the back of his wrist, in blue script, was tattooed the name *Marty*.

"We need to ask him a couple of questions about some people," Paul said.

"I do hot top, you know. I put a nice driveway in your yard, put a nice sealer on it. Charge you a fair price. That's what I do. I don't go around answering questions about nobody. Gets you in trouble."

"Sure," Paul said. "I understand that, but I'm looking for my mother, and your sister said you might know something."

"My sister?"

"Caitlin," Paul said. "She said you might be able to help us."

The pit bull kept up his very low rumbling growl.

"What makes you think I got a sister named Caitlin?"

"Well," Paul said, "you've got *Marty* tattooed on your left wrist. I took a sort of guess based on that."

"Smart guy," Marty said.

"Smart enough not to tattoo his name on his arm if he doesn't want people to know it," I said.

"Lot of guys named Marty," he said.

Paul didn't say anything. Neither did I. The dog kept growling. Marty looked at me.

"You a cop?"

"Sort of," I said.

"What the hell is sort of a cop?"

"Private detective," I said.

Marty shook his head. "Caitlin," he said. "The queen of the yuppies. What the fuck kind of name is that for an Italian broad, Caitlin?"

Paul started to speak. I shook my head. We waited.

"I don't know nothing about nobody's mother," Marty said.

"Patty Giacomin," Paul said.

"That your old lady?"

"Yes."

"Hey, that's a good paisano name."

Paul nodded. "Her boyfriend is Rich Beaumont."

Marty grinned. "Hey," he said. "Richie."

"You know him?"

"Sure. Richie's my main man."

"We think he and my mother have gone off together," Paul said, "and we're trying to find them."

58

"Hey, if she went off with Richie, she's having a good time. Why not leave them be?"

"We just want to know that she's okay," Paul said.

"She's with Richie, kid, she's okay. Hell, she probably..."

"Probably what?"

"Nothing. I forgot for a minute she's your mother, you know?"

"You know where they might be?" I said.

Marty shrugged. To do so, he had to let go of the dog. I shrugged my left shoulder slightly to feel the pleasant weight of the Browning under my arm. The dog maintained the steady sound. Maybe he was bored. Maybe he was humming to himself.

"Hell, no."

"You know where Beaumont lives?"

"Sure. Lives on the beach in Revere. One of them new condos."

"Address?"

"Richie won't like it, me giving you his address."

"We won't like it if you don't," I said.

"You getting tough with me, buddy, you like to wrestle with Buster here?"

"Buster's overmatched," I said, "unless he's carrying."

"What's that dog you got, a Doberman?"

I grinned. "Not quite," I said. "What's Rich Beaumont's address?"

Marty hesitated.

"You got all the proper licenses here?" I said. "I don't see any on that hound, for instance. You got the proper permits for everything? Asphalt storage? Vehicle's been inspected lately? That Quonset built to code?"

"Hey," Marty said. "Hey. What the fuck?"

59

"It'll save us a little time if you give us the address," Paul said. "We can find it anyway. Just take a little longer. You save us some time, we'd be very grateful. We won't tell him where we got it."

Marty looked down at the dog, looked at me, and looked back at Paul. "Sure," he said. "You seem like a nice kid." He gave Paul an address on Revere Beach Blvd. Then he looked at me. "You catch more flies with honey," he said, "than you do with vinegar. You know?"

"I've heard that," I said. "I've not found it to be true."

10

Rich Beaumont wasn't home. He had a condominium on the top floor of a twelve-story concrete building full of condominia that faced the Atlantic, across Revere Beach. From his living room you could probably see the oil tankers easing into Chelsea Creek. Rich wasn't the only one that wasn't home. Still and clean and smelling strongly of recently cured concrete, the place echoed with emptiness.

"They must have built this place as the condo boom was peaking," Paul said.

"Or slightly after," I said.

Pearl skittered down the empty corridor ahead of us, her claws sliding on the new vinyl. At the elevator she pressed her nose at the crack where the closed doors met and snuffled loudly.

"I thought she only pointed birds," Paul said.

The elevator arrived, the doors opened, and we got in. When we got to the lobby there were two guys in it. One of them was a stocky guy with a high black pompadour. He had on a black, thigh-length leather coat and black pegged pants. His black boots were badly worn at the heels and had sharp toes. The other guy was a slugger. Maybe three hundred pounds, his chin sunk into the folds of fat around his neck. Pearl went directly to them, her tail wagging, her ears pricked, her tongue lolling happily. The slugger backed up involuntarily.

"Watch it," he said to the guy with the hairdo. "That's a Doberman, it'll take your hand off."

The guy with the pompadour barely glanced at him. He put one hand down absently and scratched Pearl behind the ear.

"You the guys looking for Richie Beaumont?" he said.

I looked at Paul. "Now you say, 'Who wants to know?' "

"Who wants to know?" Paul said.

"Good," I said. "Now you." I pointed at Pompadour.

"What are you, a comedian?" he said.

"Breaking the kid in," I said. "I'd appreciate if you answered right. Say, *I want to know.*"

The fat slugger was looking nervously at Pearl. She turned her head toward him and he flinched a little, and put his hand inside his *Members Only* windbreaker.

"Listen, asshole. Vinnie Morris is outside and he wants to talk with you. Now."

"We can do this easy or hard," Sluggo said.

"Careful I don't sic my Doberman on you," I said.

"It ain't a fucking Doberman," Pompadour said, "it's a fucking pointer. Tiny don't know shit from dogs."

"Among other things," I said. "We'll talk with Vinnie."

I put Pearl's leash on and we went out through the wide glass doors and down the empty capacious steps. The light had the brightness of nearby ocean in it, and there was traffic moving on the boulevard. In the turnaround in front of the near empty condominium complex a white

Lincoln Town Car was parked. When we reached it, the rear window went down, and there was Vinnie. He still had the thick black mustache, but his hair was shorter now. He still dressed like a *GQ* cover boy.

"What the hell is that on the end of the leash?" he said. "You finally get married?"

"That's Pearl," I said. "This is Paul Giacomin. Vinnie Morris. You still with Joe, Vinnie?"

"You been trying to find Richie Beaumont," Vinnie said.

"Actually we've been trying to find Patty Giacomin," I said. "Beaumont is her boyfriend."

"Why you want her?"

"She's my mother," Paul said.

Vinnie nodded. "She sort of took off on you, huh? And didn't tell you where she was going."

"Yes," Paul said. "Or not. I don't know where she is."

"And you're looking for Richie because he's her boyfriend and you figure he'll know?"

Paul nodded.

"You know Richie Beaumont?" Vinnie said.

"No."

Vinnie nodded again and sucked on his upper lip a little.

"And if you knew where he was you wouldn't be here looking for him."

Neither Paul nor I said anything. Vinnie nodded again, to himself. At the end of the nod he jerked his head at the two soldiers. The guy with the pompadour started around the car toward the driver's side. The slugger made a circle around Pearl as he got in his side.

"I'll bet you never had a puppy as a kid," I said to him.

"Tiny never was a kid," Vinnie said. "You gonna be in your office today?"

"Could be," I said. "Any special time?"

Vinnie looked at his watch. "This afternoon, around four."

"I'll be there," I said.

Vinnie reached his hand out the rear window toward Pearl, who promptly licked it. Vinnie looked at her a moment and shook his head. He took the show handkerchief out of the breast pocket of his dark suit and wiped his hands. The car started up and pulled away, and as it went the tinted rear window eased silently up.

"You care to comment on any of this?" Paul said.

"The two enlisted men don't count. Vinnie Morris is Joe Broz's executive officer. Joe Broz is a crook."

"A crook."

"A major league, nationally known, well-connected crook," I said.

"Well, isn't this getting worse and worse," Paul said.

"Maybe," I said.

"Why are they interested in my mother?"

"I think they're interested in her for the same reason we're interested in Beaumont."

"They're looking for him."

I nodded.

"Why did he want you to be in your office later?"

"He wants to talk with me after he's talked with Joe."

"Mind if I am there?" Paul said.

I shrugged. "I hate an astute kid," I said.

"I shouldn't be there."

"No."

"Because he's got stuff to say about my mother he doesn't want me to hear."

"Probably."

"We should have insisted he say what he had to say."

"Vinnie's hard to insist," I said.

I could see the chill of realization dart through him. I knew the feeling.

"Jesus," he said. "What is she into?"

"Maybe nothing," I said. "Maybe just a boyfriend who will turn out to be sleazy."

"It would be consistent," Paul said.

Pearl had discovered a gum wrapper and was busy sniffing it from all possible perspectives.

"Can we go back to your office and call him now?"

"No," I said.

"But I want to know. I don't want to wait."

"This is a business, like most businesses it has its own rules. We let him call me at the office around four."

"That doesn't make any sense," Paul said. "Why do we have to sweat all afternoon out for some goddamned rules of the game?"

"Look," I said. "Vinnie and I have a kind of working relation, despite the fact that we are, you might say, sworn enemies. Vinnie will do what he says he will do, and so will I. He knows it, and I know it, and we can function that way. It is in our best interest to keep it that way."

"This sucks," Paul said.

Pearl picked up the gum wrapper and chewed it experimentally, and found it without savor and spit it out.

"It often does," I said.

11

At four o'clock the fall sun was glinting off the maroon scaffolding of the new building across Berkeley Street. I used to be able to sit in my office and watch the art director in a large ad agency work at her board. But Linda Thomas was gone, and so was the building, and a new skyscraper was going in, which would help to funnel the wind off the river and increase its velocity as it whistled past Police Headquarters two blocks south. I was watching the ironworkers on the scaffolding and thinking about Linda Thomas when Vinnie Morris came in exactly on time, without knocking.

He'd changed his clothes. This morning it had been a black suit with a pale blue chalk stripe. Now it was an olive brown Harris Tweed jacket, with a tattersall shirt and a rust-colored knit tie, with a wide knot. His slacks were charcoal. His kiltie loafers were mahogany cordovan. His wool socks were rust. I knew he was carrying, but his clothes were so well tailored that I couldn't tell where.

"You got the piece in the small of your back?" I said. "So it won't break the line of your jacket?"

"Yeah."

66

"It will take you an extra second to get it. Vanity will kill you sometime, Vinnie."

"Hasn't so far," Vinnie said. "The kid hire you?"

"No," I said. "It's personal."

"You and the kid or you and the old lady?"

"The kid. He's like family. The old lady doesn't matter to me except as she matters to the kid."

Vinnie was silent. I waited.

"I talked this over with Joe," Vinnie said. I waited some more. Vinnie didn't need prompting.

Vinnie shook his head and almost smiled. "He can't fucking stand you," he said.

"A tribute," I said, "to years of effort."

"But he left it up to me what I tell you, what I don't."

Vinnie was gazing past my shoulder out over Berkeley Street; there was a slice of sky you could see from that angle, to the right of the new building, and up, before the buildings closed you off across the street.

"We got an interest in Richie Beaumont."

I nodded.

A look of nearly concealed distaste showed at the corners of his mouth for a moment. "He's a friend of Joe's kid."

"Joe deserves Gerry," I said.

"I ain't here to talk about it," Vinnie said. "Gerry brought Rich in and gave him some responsibility."

"And . . . ?"

"And it didn't work out."

"And Rich dropped out of sight," I said.

"Yeah."

"Maybe with some property that Joe feels is not rightfully his."

"Yeah."

"And then you heard I was looking for him."

Vinnie was nodding slowly.

"Martinelli called you."

"Somebody called somebody, don't matter who."

"And you thought I might know something useful. So you collected the two galoots and went to meet me at the condo."

"Okay," Vinnie said. "You got everything we know. Now what do you know?"

"I got nowhere near what you know," I said. "What did Beaumont take that belongs to you? Money? Something he can use for blackmail? What were he and Gerry involved in? It had to be bad. Anything Gerry's involved in would make a buzzard puke."

"You figure Richie took off with this Giacomin broad?" Vinnie said.

"Don't know," I said. "She's not around. Thought it was logical to see if she was with her boyfriend."

"He's not around," Vinnie said.

"Un huh," I said. My repartee grew more elegant with every passing year.

"You got a thought where he might be?"

"Un uh," I said.

Vinnie sat back a little and looked at me. He had one knee crossed over the other and he tossed his foot for a moment while he looked.

"You used to be a mouthy bastard," he said finally.

"Brevity is the soul of wit," I said.

"Why's the kid want to find her?" Vinnie said.

I shrugged. "She's not around."

"So what?" Vinnie said. "My old lady's not around either. I ain't looking for her."

"He cares about her," I said.

"There's one difference right there," Vinnie said. "She got something he wants?"

"His past," I said.

Vinnie looked at me some more, and tossed his foot some more.

"His past," Vinnie said.

I nodded.

"What the fuck is that supposed to mean?"

"Kid's about to get married," I said. "She was pretty much a bitch all his childhood and he wants to know her as something other than that before he moves too far on into adulthood."

"You shoulda been a college professor," Vinnie said.

"You say that because you don't know any college professors," I said.

Vinnie shrugged. "Anyway, that may all be true, whatever the fuck it means, but it don't help my case. Or, far as I can see, yours."

"True," I said. "But you asked me."

"Yeah," Vinnie said. "Sure. The point is you're looking and we're looking and I want to be sure we aren't trampling on each other's feet, you know?"

He took a package of Juicy Fruit gum from his coat pocket and offered me some. I shook my head, and he selected a stick, and peeled it open, and folded it into his mouth.

"Me and Joe don't give a fuck about her," he said. "We want him."

"I don't give a fuck about him," I said. "I want her."

Vinnie smiled widely. "Perfect," he said and chewed his gum slowly.

"How about Gerry?" I said.

69

This time there was no hint of expression in Vinnie's face. "Hey, he's Joe's kid."

"Joe's a creep," I said, "but compared to his kid he's Abraham Lincoln."

Vinnie turned his hands palms up.

"Is Gerry going to get in the way?" I said.

"Joe told him to stay out of this."

"You think he will?"

Again Vinnie's face was without expression. His voice was entirely neutral.

"No."

"Like I said. What about Gerry?"

"Okay," Vinnie said. "We won't fuck around with this either. I been with Joe a long time. You don't like him. That's okay. He don't like you. But Joe says he'll do something, he will. He says he won't, he won't."

"That's true for you, Vinnie. It's not true for Joe."

"We won't argue. I know Joe a long time. But we both know Gerry and we know he's a fucking ignoramus."

"But he's mean and you can't trust him," I said.

"Exactly," Vinnie said. "And Joe loves him. Joe don't see him for the fucking weasel that he is."

"So you're going to have trouble with Gerry too."

"Nothing I can't handle."

"Tricky though," I said.

"Yeah," Vinnie said.

"You want to tell me what kind of mess Gerry is in with Richie Beaumont?"

"No."

The light was beginning to fade outside, and the traffic sounds drifting up from Boylston Street increased as people started going home. The ironworkers had already left the site where Linda Thomas had worked once, across the

70

street, and the maroon skeleton stood empty. Bare ruined choirs where late the sweet birds sang.

"I have no interest in Richie Beaumont," I said. "But I have a lot of interest in Patty Giacomin. I would not want anything bad to happen to her."

"I got no need to hurt the old lady," Vinnie said.

"You let me know if you find her?"

"You let me know if you find him?"

I grinned. "Maybe."

"Yeah," Vinnie said. "Me too."

We were silent some more, listening to the traffic.

"I don't want trouble with you, Spenser."

"Who would," I said.

"You're probably half as good as you think you are," Vinnie said. "But that's pretty good. And you got re-sources."

"Hawk," I said.

"You and he can be a large pain in the fungones."

"Nice of you to say so, Vinnie. Hawk will be flattered."

"So let's think about helping each other out, maybe, to the extent we can."

"Sure," I said.

"Good," Vinnie said. Then he stood up and headed for the door. At the door he paused, and then turned slowly back.

"Hawk with you in this?" he said.

"Not so far," I said.

"Gerry's got a lot at stake here," Vinnie said. He looked down, and without looking up said, "Kid's a back-shooter."

"He has to be," I said. "Thanks."

Vinnie was still looking at the floor. He nodded.

"Yeah," he said. And went out.

12

Susan insisted on cooking dinner for Paul and me. When she put her mind to it she could cook, but she had a lot of trouble putting her mind to it, and most of the time she had it delivered from The Harvest Express.

"Helmut hears you're doing your own cooking," I said, "he'll have a heart attack. You represent his profit margin."

"I won't abandon him," Susan said. She had every pot she owned, including two she had just bought for the occasion, out on the counter. Pearl was underfoot sampling the residue in a pan already used. Susan gave us each a Catamount Golden Lager to drink and then went back to her preparation.

"Couscous," she said. "With chicken and vegetables."

"Sounds great," Paul said.

Susan cleared a space among the pans and put some chicken breasts down on the marble counter and began to cut them into cubes. Pearl stood on her hind legs, with her front paws on the counter, and pointed the raw chicken from a distance of three inches.

"Doesn't that tend to beat hell out of the knife blade?" Paul said.

Susan looked at him as if he'd espoused pedophilia.

"No," Paul said quickly. "No, of course it doesn't."

I sipped my beer. Susan continued to hack up the chicken. She had her lower lip caught in her teeth, as she always did when she was concentrating. I liked to watch her.

Paul watched me watching her.

"Is Susan the first woman you ever loved?" he said.

"Yes."

"What about this hussy you mentioned the other day in the Ritz Bar?" asked Susan.

"She was a girl," I said.

"And you?" Susan said.

"I was sixteen," I said. "And she sat in front of me in French class."

"Sixteen?" Paul said. "You had a childhood?"

Pearl managed to get a scrap of raw chicken. She got down quickly and trotted to the living room where she put it on the rug and rolled on it.

"I can hardly remember her face now," I said. "But she had long hair the color of thyme honey, and she combed it straight back and it was quite long and very smooth. Her name was Dale Carter, and I used to write her little notes of poetry and slip them to her. And she'd read them and smile and I knew she was flattered."

"Poetry?" Susan said.

Pearl returned from the living room licking her muzzle.

"Yeah. Stuff I'd read and would adjust to fit her. *Dale, thy beauty is to me like those Nicean barks of yore* . . . that kind of thing."

Paul and Susan looked at each other. Pearl continued to point the chicken.

"Well," Susan said, "you were sixteen."

"Barely," I said.

"So," she said, "did it develop?"

"We became friends," I said. "We would talk all the time between classes and we would eat lunch together and sit on the high school steps after school, and I just couldn't get enough of her. I just wanted to look at her and hear her voice."

Paul was sitting quietly, watching me. There was no amusement in his face.

"She was slender," I said. "Medium height, from a well-off and intellectual family in the Back Bay. Very, ah, Brahmin. And there was something about her way of carrying herself. She seemed to walk very lightly. She seemed to be very, very interested in what you said, and she would listen with her lips just a little apart and breathe softly through her mouth while she listened."

Susan wet her lower lip and opened her mouth and leaned forward and panted at me.

"A little more subtly than that," I said. "And she would sort of cock her head a little to the side when she talked and look right at me."

Susan tossed her chicken into a bowl and poured some honey over it, and sprinkled on some spices. Pearl's eyes had never left the chicken. When it went in the bowl her eyes didn't leave the bowl.

"Did you go out?" Susan said.

"Not really," I said. "They used to have sort of a canteen dance every afternoon after school in the basement of the Legion hall across the street. Some sort of keep-the-kids-off-the-street campaign which lasted about six months.

74

And we used to go over there sometimes and dance. I never danced very well."

"I'll say," Susan murmured.

"But with her I was Arthur Murray. She seemed to operate a little off the ground, as if her feet were floating; and her hand on my shoulder was very light and yet she felt every movement of the music and seemed to know exactly where I was going before I went. And she always wore perfume. And good clothes. I don't even remember what they were like, but I knew they were good."

"Longish skirt," Susan said. "Thick white socks halfway up the calf, penny loafers, cashmere sweater, maybe a little white collar like Dorothy Collins on *The Hit Parade.*"

"Yeah," I said. "That's exactly right."

"Of course it is. It's what I wore. It's what we all wore, those of us who wore 'good clothes.' "

Paul's attention, I noticed peripherally, had intensified. Pearl had moved out of the kitchen, encouraged by a gentle shove from Susan, and now sat on the floor beside my stool, her shoulder leaning in against my leg, her eyes still fixed on the bowl where the chicken was marinating.

"Sure," I said. "Anyway we'd dance sometimes, and dance close, but no kissing, or protestations of affection, except cloaked as badinage. I never took her out in the sense of going to her house, picking her up, taking her to the movies, to a dance, that stuff. We never had a meal together except in the school cafeteria."

"Why didn't you take her out, kiss her, take her to dinner?"

"Shy."

"Shy?" Susan said. "You?"

"When I was a kid," I said. "I was shy with girls."

75

"And now you're not."

"No," I said, "now I'm not."

Susan was struggling with the seal on a box of prepackaged couscous.

Pearl was leaning more heavily against my leg, her neck stretched as far as she could stretch it, to rest her head on my thigh.

"Well, weren't you weird," Susan said.

"It's great talking to a professional psychotherapist," I said. "They are so sensitive, so aware of human motivation, so careful to avoid stereotypic labeling."

"Yes, weirdo," Susan said. "We take pride in that. What happened to her?"

Paul reached over to pat Pearl's head. Pearl misread it as a food offer and snuffled at his open palm, and finding no food, settled for lapping Paul's hand. Susan got the box of couscous open and dumped it in another bowl and added some water.

"She told me one day that a close friend of mine had asked her to the junior class dance, and should she accept."

"And of course you told her yes, she should accept," Susan said. "Because that was the honorable thing to do."

"I said yes, that she should accept."

"Now that you are sophisticated and no longer shy with girls, I assume you understand that she was asking you if you were going to ask her to the dance, and was telling you that if you were, she would turn your friend down and go with you."

"I now understand that," I said. "But consider if I had been different. What if I had not panted after the sweet sorrow of renunciation? What if I'd gone to the dance with her, and we'd become lovers and married and lived happily ever after? What would have become of you?"

"I don't know," Susan said. "I guess I'd have wandered the world tragically, wearing my polka dot panties, looking for Mister Right, never knowing that Mister Right had married his high school sweetheart."

Paul put his hands over his ears.

"Polka dot panties?" he said.

Susan smiled. She transferred the refreshed couscous from the bowl to a cook pot. Neither Paul nor I asked her why she had not refreshed it in the cook pot in the first place. She put the cook pot on the stove and put a lid on it and turned the flame on low.

I rested my hand on Pearl's head. "I think," I said, "that even had Dale and I gone to the dance and lived happily ever after, we wouldn't have lived happily ever after. Any more than you were able to stay with your first husband."

"Because we'd have been looking for each other?"

I nodded.

"That's what you think, isn't it?" Susan said. She was no longer teasing me.

"Yes," I said. "That's what I think. I think your marriage broke up because you weren't married to me. I think neither one of us could be happy with anyone else because we would always be looking for each other, without even knowing it, without knowing who each other was or even knowing there was an each other."

"Do you think that's true of love in general?"

"No," I said. "I only believe that about us."

"Isn't that kind of exclusionary?" Paul said.

"Yes," I said. "Embarrassingly so."

The room was silent now, not the light and airy silence of contentment, but the weighty silence of intensity.

Paul was choosing his words very carefully. It took him a little time.

"But you're not saying I couldn't feel that way?"

"No," I said. "I'm not."

Paul nodded. I could see him thinking some more.

"Do you feel that way?" I said.

"I don't know," he said. "And I feel like I ought to, because you do."

"No need to be like me," I said.

"Who else, then?" he said. "Who would I be like? My father? Who did I learn to be me from?"

"You're right," I said. "I was glib. But you know as well as I do that you can't spend your life feeling as I do, and thinking what I think. You don't now."

"The way you love her makes me feel inadequate," Paul said. "I don't think I can love anyone like that."

Susan was chopping fresh mint on the marble countertop.

"One love at a time," she said.

"Which means what?" Paul said. "My mother?"

Susan smiled her Freudian smile. "We shrinks always imply more than we say."

"There's nothing necessarily bizarre in wanting to find my mother."

"Of course not, and when you do it will help clarify things, maybe."

"Maybe," Paul said.

I sipped a little more of my Catamount Gold and thought about Dale Carter, whom I hadn't seen in so long. It wasn't the first time I'd thought about her. I looked at Susan. She smiled at me, a wholly non-Freudian smile.

"We'd have found each other," she said.

"In fact," I said, "we did it twice."

13

Hawk, wearing white satin sweatpants and no shirt, was hanging upside down in gravity boots in the Harbor Health Club, doing sit-ups. He curled his body up parallel with the floor and eased it back vertical without any apparent effort. The abdominus rictus tightened and relaxed under his shiny black skin. He had his hands clasped loosely behind his head, and the skin over his biceps seemed too tight.

Around him men and women in bright spandex were working out with varying success. All of them and two of the three trainers that Henry Cimoli employed were glancing covertly at Hawk. His upper body and his shaved head were shiny with sweat. But his breath was easy and there was no other indication that what he was doing might be hard.

I said, "You stuck on that apparatus, boy?"

Hawk grinned upside down and did another sit-up.

"Damn," he said. "Can't seem to reach my feet."

He put out his hand upside down and I gave him an understated low five.

"When you get through struggling with that thing," I said, "I'll buy you breakfast."

"Sure," Hawk said.

We worked out for maybe an hour and a half, and took a little steam afterwards. Then, showered and dressed and fragrant with the cheap after-shave that Henry put out in the men's locker room, we strolled out across Atlantic Avenue toward Quincy Market. It was still early in the day, only 9:30, and the autumn sun was mild as it slanted down at us, only a few degrees up over the harbor, and made our shadows long and angular ahead of us.

"Market's nice this time of day," Hawk said.

"Yeah," I said. "Hasn't turned into a five-acre dating bar yet."

"Get a chance to meet a lot of interesting people from Des Moines," Hawk said. "After lunch."

"And some dandy teenagers in from the subs," I said.

We sat at the counter in the nearly quiet central market building. I had some blueberry pancakes. Hawk had four scrambled eggs and toast. We each ordered coffee.

"I thought you quit coffee," Hawk said.

"I changed my mind," I said.

"Couldn't do it, huh?"

"Decided not to," I said and put a spoonful of sugar in and stirred and drank some carefully. Life began again. Behind us along the central aisle the food stalls prepared for the day. One would never starve to death in Quincy Market. Behind us was a shop selling roast goose sandwiches. To our right was an oyster bar. A few tourists strolled through early, wearing cameras, and new Red Sox hats made of plastic mesh that fit badly. Mixed in was an occasional secretary on coffee break, and now and then, resplendently garbed, and moving with great alacrity, were young brokers from the financial district picking up a special blend coffee for the big meeting.

"You have any information on what Gerry Broz is doing these days?" I said.

"No," Hawk said. "You?"

"No, but it involves a guy named Rich Beaumont, who is Patty Giacomin's current squeeze."

"Anything Gerry involved in is not a good thing."

"This is true," I said. "She's missing. Paul wants to find her."

"How 'bout Beaumont?"

"Missing too," I said.

"Un huh."

"Exactly," I said. "You tribal types are so wise."

"We close to nature," Hawk said. The counterman came by and refilled our coffee cups. I managed to stay calm.

"You talk to Vinnie?" Hawk said.

"He talked to me. Wants to be sure we don't get in each other's way."

"He tell you what Gerry doing?"

"No."

"Vinnie can't stand him any more than you or me."

"I know," I said. "But he's Joe's kid."

Hawk drank some coffee. Like everything else he did, it seemed easier for him. The coffee was not too hot. He seemed to drink it the way it had been drawn up, perfectly, without any effort. I'd seen him kill people the same way.

"Joe's damn near as bad as the kid," Hawk said. "Vinnie's what keeps the outfit together."

"Vinnie'd be better off without him," I said.

"Vinnie don't think so," Hawk said.

"I know."

"He been with Joe a long time. Since he been a kid."

"Yeah."

A woman with too much blonde hair went past us wearing stretch jeans and very high heels that caused her hips to sway when she walked. Hawk and I watched her all the way down the length of the market until she turned aside in the rotunda and we lost her.

"Stretch fabric is a good thing," I said.

"We going to talk with Gerry?" Hawk said.

"I thought we might," I said.

Hawk nodded and pushed the last of his scrambled eggs onto his fork with the last of his toast. He put the eggs very delicately into his mouth and followed with the toast. He chewed carefully and swallowed and picked up his cup and drank some coffee. He put the cup down, picked up his napkin, and patted his lips.

"Don't sound like you got anybody else to talk to," he said.

"Nope."

"Paul worried about her?"

"Yes."

He nodded. "Want me to see I can arrange it?" he said.

I drank more of my second cup. "Soon as I finish my coffee," I said.

14

Paul and I went back to see Martinelli. He wasn't there and the shop was closed. We went back to see his sister Caitlin. She wasn't there. And she wasn't there the next day when we called, nor that evening, nor the next morning. And neither was Martinelli. We went back to the real estate women at *Chez Vous.* They had nothing to add. They didn't know anyone else who would have anything to add. They seemed to know less than when I'd spoken to them first. We talked with three other people we'd tracked down through the answering machine. They didn't know who Rich Beaumont was. They didn't know where Patty might be. At least two sort of hinted that they also didn't care. We called every travel agent in the Yellow Pages and every major airline without success. There was no business listing for Rich Beaumont in the Yellow Pages. The Secretary of State's office had no listing of any company with that name in its title. Nobody at either North or South Station could help us. Nobody at either bus terminal could help us. I got Beaumont's registration number, make, and model from the Registry. There was no car that fit the plate or description parked in the garage of the Revere Beach condo or anywhere around. None had been towed by either Boston or MDC police.

"It looks like they disappeared on purpose," Paul said.

We were walking Pearl along the river, past the lagoon, west of the Hatch Shell. Some ducks were cruising the lagoon, and when Pearl spotted them she got lower and longer and sucked in her stomach and froze in a quivering point. Paul and I stopped and let her point for a moment.

"Yeah, but it doesn't have to mean that. They could simply have gotten in his car and driven off in full innocence. We'd have come up with same zero."

Pearl edged a step closer to the ducks. Her complete self was invested in them. I picked up a small rock and tossed it at them. They rose from the water and swept out toward the river. I said, "Bang," and Pearl broke the point and glanced at me for a moment and then forgot about it and proceeded on, her nose close to the ground, tracking the elusive candy wrapper.

"What about the fact that we can't find either of the two people who had anything useful to tell us?" Paul said.

"Not encouraging," I said.

"Do you think anything happened to them?"

"Probably not," I said. "Probably they were told to go away for a while and they did."

"Joe Broz?"

I shrugged.

"The son, whatsisname?"

"Gerry," I said. "No way to know yet."

"So now what do we do?" Paul said. "A tearful plea on the noon news?"

"Let's hold off a little on that," I said. "Let's go out to Lexington and collect your mother's mail."

"Can you do that?"

"You can," I said. "Just tell them your mother wanted you to pick it up for her. If some postal clerk is really zealous you can prove you're her son."

We finished Pearl's walk, in which she pointed a flock of pigeons, and tracked down the wrapper to a Zagnut Bar, and went back to my place and loaded her into the car and headed out to Lexington.

The postal clerk was the same woman with the teased pink hair that I'd talked with before, though she didn't seem to remember me.

"You talk to your mother's friend?" she said when Paul presented himself.

"No," he said.

"Oh. I figured when we couldn't give him the mail he got hold of you."

"No, my mother didn't mention it," Paul said.

"I hate regulations, too," the clerk said. "But they're there. You can't just hand the mail out to anyone who asks."

"Sure," Paul said. "It's a good rule."

"Yeah." She shrugged. "Well, some people get pretty mean about it, but I don't make the rules, you know?"

"I know, you did the right thing."

"But since you're her son, no problem."

Paul nodded encouragingly.

"We should tell him we've got the mail," I said to Paul. He nodded. I looked at the clerk.

"You wouldn't know who he was, would you?"

"Gee, I have no idea," she said. "Sort of a short guy, lot of hair, combed up in front, like Elvis. Only he's real dark, like a dago or a Frenchman."

I looked at Paul. "Sounds like Uncle Nick," I said.

"Yeah, Nicky's really excitable."

"Well, I don't care if he's your uncle or not. He was mean as hell. He had some ID, he should have shown it to me."

"He's not really my uncle," Paul said. "Just an old friend of my mother's. We call him Uncle Nick."

"Well, he's a mean one," the clerk said.

There were four or five people forming in line behind us at the single window. One of them said something about "social hour" to his line mate. The clerk ignored them.

"We don't get paid enough to take abuse, you know what I'm saying."

"I hear you," Paul said with a straight face.

Behind us the line was shuffling and clearing its various throats. Paul glanced at his watch.

"Wow," he said. "It's late. I didn't realize. We better stop wasting this lady's time."

"Hey," the clerk said. "No problem. We're here every day, serving the public. You're not wasting my time."

Someone in the line said something about *"my* time."

"Well, thanks," Paul said. "I really appreciate it. We better just grab the mail and get rolling." He looked at his watch again and shook his head, *Where does the time go?* The clerk nodded understandingly and strolled slowly back of the partition and was gone maybe two minutes and returned with a bundle of mail held together by large rubber bands. She handed it to Paul. He smiled. I smiled. The clerk smiled. The rest of the line shuffled a little more and shifted its feet. We took the mail and left.

Pearl was sitting in the driver's seat, as she always was

when left alone. She insinuated herself into the backseat the minute she saw us coming, and was in perfect position to lap me behind the ear when I got in the car.

"Brilliant," I said to Paul. "Brilliantly charming, and no hint of eagerness. Masterful."

"I am, after all, a performer," Paul said. "I assume the guy that came asking was that short one we saw in Revere, the one with the huge fat pal, the ones with Vinnie Morris."

"I assume," I said. "Means Vinnie is getting nowhere too."

Paul had the mail in his lap. He handed it to me.

"I don't feel right reading her mail," he said. "What if there's letters there with stuff in them I don't want to see?"

"Love letters?"

"Yeah, explicit stuff. You know? *'I'm still thinking about when I bleeped your bleep.'* You want to read stuff like that about your mother?"

"Remember," I said, "I never had one."

"Yes, I forget that sometimes."

We were quiet for a while.

"Mothers are never only mothers," I said.

"I know," Paul said. "Christ, do I know. I've had ten years of psychotherapy. I know shit like that better than I want to. I still don't want to read about my mother boinking some jerk."

I nodded.

"I don't know why I should worry about *reading* it," Paul said. "She's probably been *doing* it since puberty."

I nodded again. I always thought people had the right to boink who they wanted, even a jerk, if they needed to.

88

But that probably wasn't really Paul's issue and shutting up never seemed to do much harm.

"I'll read the mail," I said.

Most of it could be dispensed with unread: catalogues, magazines, direct mail advertising. Paul took the batch and walked across the parking lot and dumped it in a trash barrel. The rest were bills, no boinking. The bills produced nothing much, except finally, the very last entry on her American Express bill, a clothing store in Lenox. I turned to the individual receipts and located it. Tailored Lady, Lenox, Massachusetts, Lingerie. It was dated after her mail had been put on hold. I handed it to Paul.

"Know anything about this?"

"No," he said. "All I know about Lenox is the Berkshires, Tanglewood. I don't think I've ever been there."

"That your mother's signature?" I said.

"Looks like her writing. I rarely see her signature. When I got money it was usually a check from my father. But it looks like her writing."

"So," I said. "She was probably in Lenox ten days ago."

"Should we go out there?"

"Yes," I said. "We should. But first Hawk and I want to speak with Gerry Broz."

"About my mother?"

"Yeah."

"Both of you?"

"It's always nice to have backup when you talk with Gerry."

"For god's sake what is she mixed up in when even you need backup to talk to people about her?"

"Doesn't need to be awful," I said. "She probably doesn't even know Gerry."

"Well, it sounds awful and everything we learn about it makes it sound worse."

"We'll find out," I said. "In a while we'll know whatever there is to know."

"I'm getting scared," Paul said. "Scared for her."

"Sure you are," I said. "I would if I were you."

"I don't like being scared."

"Nobody does," I said.

"But everybody is," Paul said.

"At one time or another," I said.

"You?"

"Sure."

"Hawk?"

I paused. "I don't know," I said. "You never can be sure with Hawk."

15

Pearl looked painfully resentful as Susan and I left her. Susan had left the television tuned to CNN.

"She likes to watch Catherine Crier," Susan said.

"Me too."

"More than Diane Sawyer?"

"Well, of course not," I said.

Susan had recently acquired one of those turbocharged Japanese sports cars, which she drove like a New York cabbie, flooring it between stoplights and talking trash to other motorists. We made the fifteen-minute drive from Susan's place to Icarus Restaurant in about seven minutes. And gave the car to the valet kid and went in.

Icarus is very voguish and demure and the sight of Hawk waiting for us at a table was enough to cheer me for the evening. He looked like a moose at a gazelle convention. He stood when he saw Susan and she kissed him. There was a bottle of Krug in an ice bucket beside the table. When we sat, Hawk took it from the ice, wiped it with the towel, and poured champagne into Susan's glass then mine.

Susan raised her glass and said, "To us." We clinked and

drank. The corners of Susan's eyes were crinkled with amusement.

"I can't tell you," she said, "how out of place you two look in here."

"Not our fault we big," Hawk said.

"Of course not," Susan said. "Have you seen pictures of Pearl?"

"Not yet," Hawk said.

Susan rummaged in her purse. Which was quite tricky, since the purse wasn't much bigger than a postcard. She was wearing a white suit with gold braid and epaulets, and she seemed, as she always did, to occupy the center of the room. Everything else seemed to group around her and be ordered by her, like a jar in Tennessee. When you were with Susan you could remain anonymous. No one would notice you.

Even Hawk was less apparent when he was with Susan.

Tonight he was all in black. Suit, shirt, tie. I was even more daring in a blue blazer, tan slacks, a white oxford button-down shirt, and a maroon tie with tiny white dots in it.

"You the world's oldest preppie," Hawk said to me. "You got on wing-tipped cordovans?"

"Like hell," I said and stuck my foot out so he could check the loafers. "Note the stunning little kiltie, as well as the hint of a tassel."

"Probably got an argyle gun," Hawk said.

"In a chino holster," I said. "With a little belt in the back."

Susan found her folder of pictures of Pearl and put them on the table in front of Hawk. He looked at them silently as Susan provided commentary.

"There she is her first day with us," Susan said. "And there she is with her ball. There she is on the bed with himself."

Hawk looked at me. "A dog?" he said.

I shrugged. "I like dogs," I said.

Hawk nodded. "Sure you do. Known that long as I've known you."

We were silent for a moment, looking at the menu. The waiter appeared. We ordered. The waiter departed.

"How long have you known him?" Susan said to Hawk.

Hawk grinned. "You remember?" he said to me.

"Shouldn't smile like that," I said. "Spoils the monochromatic look."

"Whites of my eyes a problem there, too," Hawk said.

"*Do* you remember?" Susan said to me.

"Sure. We were fighting a prelim at the Arena."

"We on the card so early, the ushers still dusting off the seats," Hawk said.

"The Arena? That's not the Garden."

"No, the Boston Arena. These days it's a hockey rink. All cleaned up and presentable. Northeastern University owns it now."

"Did you fight each other in this preliminary bout?" Susan said.

"Yeah," I said.

"Well?" Susan said.

"Well what?" I said.

"Hawk?" Susan said.

Hawk looked at her and smiled and raised his eyebrows.

"What?" he said.

"Who won?" Susan said.

"I did," we both said simultaneously.

93

Susan stared at us for a moment and then smiled. "Of course you did," she said.

"Mostly white fighters in Boston in those days," Hawk said.

"Hawk was the great black hope," I said.

"Night me and Spenser fought, lotta people didn't like a black fighter on the card."

The first course arrived. The waiter put it down and then refreshed our champagne glasses.

"After, ah, one of us won the fight," Hawk said, "I got cleaned up and dressed and I'm coming out of the Arena and I run into a group of young white guys. They drunk. Lot of people go to the fights at the Arena are drunk. And one of them spoke loudly, and unkindly of . . . I believe the phrase was *jigaboos*. At which I took some offense."

"How many were there?" Susan said.

"Enough so they brave," Hawk said. "Six, maybe, eight. Anyway, ah expressed my resentment to the guy who had called me a jigaboo, and it caused him to spit out some of his front teeth. And so his friends jump in. Normally me against eight drunks is probably about even. But I'm a little winded from fighting your friend, and winning—"

"Losing," I said.

"And I'm beginning to give a little ground when Spenser comes out and sees the fight and jumps in on my side and their side calls him a nigger lover and Spenser throw him through a window."

"Open?" Susan said.

"No."

Susan winced.

"Who won?" Susan said. I knew she knew the answer, but she was kind enough to feed it to us.

"We did," Hawk and I said simultaneously.

Susan laughed. "I knew you would," she said. "Did you ever fight each other again?"

"No," I said.

The appetizers went away and the entree came, pork tenderloin with sour cherry sauce, and polenta. I was so pleased with it that I never even noticed what Hawk and Susan were eating.

"But you stayed in touch," Susan said.

"In a manner of speaking, Lollypop," Hawk said.

"We'd go shopping together," I said. "Take in some matinees, have a sundae at Bailey's, after."

"I feel that I am being made sport of," Susan said, "by a pair of sexist oinkers."

"You got that right," Hawk said.

"How did you stay in touch, Porkies?"

"Our work tended to bring us in contact," Hawk said. "First when we fighting, we'd be on the same card sometime, changing in the same back room in some gym."

"And later?" Susan said.

"Our professional lives continued to intersect," I said. "Still do."

"We both involved in the matter of, ah, crime," Hawk said.

"From varying perspectives," I said.

"You are each other's best friend," Susan said. "In some genuine sense you love each other. But you never show it, never speak of it. One would never know."

"You know," Hawk said.

"Only because I know you so well."

"We know," Hawk said.

95

"And nobody else much matters," Susan said.

Hawk smiled and didn't say anything. Susan looked at him then at me.

"Peas in a pod," she said.

16

I left Pearl with Susan in the morning when Hawk picked me up in his forest green Jaguar sedan.

"She can't go with you?" Susan said.

"Hawk hates dog drool on the leather seats," I said.

"You don't care about that," Susan said. "And neither does Hawk. You think it might be dangerous going to see Gerry Broz and you don't want her to get hurt, or you to get hurt and her to be left alone." Susan was wearing a kimono with vertical black and white stripes, and she hadn't put her makeup on yet. Her face was shiny and vulnerable in its morning innocence.

"Gerry's a weird dude," I said.

She nodded and held up her face and I kissed her, and patted Pearl and went on to Hawk.

"Gonna come by someday, see a tricycle on the porch," Hawk said as he slid the Jag away from the curb in front of Susan's house.

"Maybe Paul will have a kid," I said.

"Get you one of those bumper stickers say ASK ME ABOUT MY GRANDCHILD," Hawk said.

"There's a Dunkin' Donuts in Union Square, Somerville," I said. "You could get me coffee instead."

Which we did, and drank it as we drove on 93 and 128 to Beverly. We were meeting Gerry in an Italian restaurant called Rocco's Grotto on Rantoul Street. The front of Rocco's was done in fake fieldstone. A big neon sign in the window advertised PIZZA, PASTA, & MORE. There was a bicycle repair shop next door and across the street a billiard parlor. Hawk and I got out of the car and went to the front door. There was a stock sign in the window that said CLOSED on it. I tried the door. It opened and we went in. There were booths down the left-hand wall, a bar down the right, and tables in the space between. Most of the tables had chairs upside down on them. Past the end of the bar was a swinging door to the kitchen, with a pass-through window to the left of it. Beyond that was a short corridor to the rest rooms. Behind the bar was a guy with straggly blond hair and a skinny neck. He was brewing coffee. He looked up when we came in.

"You here for Gerry?" he said.

I said yes.

He jerked his head toward a booth.

"He'll be along," he said.

He had probably been a thin guy once, but as time passed he had gotten sort of plump until the only remnant of his former self was his thin neck.

Hawk ignored the head gesture toward a booth and took the barstool nearest the kitchen. He moved it away from the kitchen door and sat on it, leaning against the back wall. I sat at the other end, near the door. No sense bunching up. The guy with the skinny neck shrugged and looked at his coffee maker. The water had nearly stopped dripping through the filter. He leaned his hips against the inside of the bar and crossed his arms and studied it as it dripped more and more occasionally. Finally it stopped altogether. The round glass pot was full.

The guy with the skinny neck got a round bar tray from under the bar and put a coffee mug on it, a small cardboard carton of heavy cream, and a bowl filled with paper packets of Equal. He put a teaspoon on the tray beside the coffee mug. Then he put the tray up on the bar top and went into the kitchen. He came back in maybe two minutes with a plate of Italian pastries. I saw raisin cake, biscotti, hazelnut cake, and cannoli. He put the plate on the tray and then he leaned back against the bar again and folded his arms again, and looked at nothing.

Which was what I was looking at.

Then the door opened and a big guy came in wearing a tan Ultrasuede thigh-length coat. He had very big hands, and even though everything seemed to fit him fine, his hands were so big that it made him look like his sleeves were too short.

He looked first at Hawk in the back, and then at me. And then moved on into the restaurant leaving the door ajar and leaned on the wall near Hawk.

Gerry Broz came in next, and after him two more bodyguards. One wore a tan corduroy sport coat over a dark brown sport shirt. The sport coat had brown leather elbow patches but fit him so badly that I could see the bulge on his right hip where he wore a gun. The other bodyguard wore a dark blue three-piece suit. He had on a blue and red figured tie with a very wide knot, and a trench coat worn like a cape over his shoulders. As he came through the front door, he reached back with his left hand and pulled it shut. Then he produced a double-barreled shotgun with the barrels sawed off and the stock modified, and held that, muzzle down, in his right hand.

"That it for backup?" I said to Gerry. "Nobody on the roof?"

"Hey, asshole, you asked for this meet," Gerry said.

"One of your many good qualities, Gerry," I said. "You are a master of the clever riposte."

The tall guy with the two big hands said from the back, "Why don't you just shut your fucking mouth."

"Barbarians," I said to Hawk. "We have fallen among barbarians." I looked at the guy behind the bar. "And this seemed like such a nice place too," I said.

He ignored me. He picked up the tray he'd prepared and went over to the booth along the left wall, near the door, where Gerry had slid in by himself. It was getting harder and harder for Gerry to slide into booths. Every time I saw him he seemed to have gained another ten. He wasn't a big guy, and he obviously didn't work out, so that every pound he packed on looked like twice that and very flabby. Moreover his wardrobe hadn't caught up to his poundage, so that everything seemed tight and you had the sense that he was very uncomfortable.

The bartender poured him some coffee, and left the pot. Gerry poured some heavy cream in, added four packets of Equal, and stirred slowly while he ate a biscotto. His hair was cut long in the back and short on top, where it was spiked. He had a camel's hair topcoat on, which he wore open with the belt hanging loose. He wasn't too much older than Paul and already there were small red veins showing on his cheeks. He swallowed the last of his first biscotto, and drank some coffee, and put the mug down.

"Okay, asshole," he said. "Hawk told Lucky you wanted

to ask me something." He nodded his head toward the guy with the sawed-off so I should know which one was Lucky.

"What are you and Rich Beaumont doing?" I said.

Nobody said anything. Gerry gazed at me without expression for a long time. The bartender cleared his throat once, softly, turning his head away and covering his mouth as if he were in church.

Finally Gerry said, "Who?"

"Rich Beaumont," I said. "You and he are involved in some kind of scam which has gone sour and now you and everybody else is looking for Rich. I want to know what the scam was."

Gerry looked at me stonily some more. It was supposed to make the marrow congeal in my bones. Then he ate a cannoli, drank some more coffee, looked around the room with what passed in Gerry's life for a big grin.

"Any you guys know Rich Beaumont?" He made a point of mispronouncing it, putting the emphasis on the first syllable.

"You, Lucky?"

The guy with the shotgun shook his head.

"Maishe?"

Maishe was the guy with the oversized hands. "Never heard of him," he said.

"Rock?"

The bartender shook his head.

"Anthony?"

"Never heard of no Rich Beaumont." The guy in the corduroy coat mispronounced Beaumont just as his boss had.

"You got any other questions, asshole?"

101

"Yeah," I said. "How many more times you think you can screw up like this before your father won't let you play anymore?"

The silence in the restaurant gathered like a fog. Gerry's face got red. His breath rasped. He leaned suddenly forward over the table. An elbow knocked over his mug and coffee puddled on the table top.

"You cocksucker," he said. "You can't talk that way to me."

"Why not?" I said. "You think these four guys are enough?"

"Nobody, nobody . . ." He seemed to run out of air and stopped and took in a deep breath.

"Lucky," he said.

The guy with the shotgun half turned toward me and suddenly there was a gun in Hawk's hand. No one had seen any movement, but there it was. Everyone froze for a moment on the big .44, with the long barrel and the hammer thumbed back.

"Gerry goes first," Hawk said.

The focus turned back to me. I had managed to get the Browning out and cocked. Lucky had the shotgun leveled at me. Maishe had a hand under his coat and Anthony stood motionless with his hand half raised toward a shoulder holster. Behind the bar Rocco's hands were out of sight. I kept the gun on Lucky. Nobody moved. It was very close quarters and if the balloon went up it was going to be a mess. I could hear Gerry's breath laboring in and out. The kitchen door swung open and Vinnie Morris walked into the dining room.

"What the fuck?" he said.

Nobody moved. Vinnie walked over to Lucky and casually put a hand on the shotgun and pushed the barrels down. Then he turned toward the booth where Gerry was sitting.

"What the fuck, Gerry?" he said. He gestured with one hand toward Maishe, and with the other toward Anthony. They let their hands drop. I put the Browning back under my arm. Hawk's gun disappeared.

"What are you doing here?" Gerry said finally.

"Joe asked me to hang around, keep an eye on things."

"He knew about this meeting?"

"Sure."

Gerry looked at the guy behind the bar.

"Rocco?" he said.

Rocco shrugged. "Joe's bar," he said.

"You fucking snitch," Gerry said.

"I work for Joe," Rocco said. "No need to give me a batch of shit about it."

"I'll give you any batch of shit I want to, you squealing cocksucker."

"Vinnie?" Rocco said.

Vinnie nodded. To Gerry he said, "Shhh."

"So my father knew. So what?" Gerry said. "What the fuck he have to send you for? He thinks I can't handle this?"

"He don't want you getting hurt," Vinnie said. "He says, Vinnie, go down, stay out of the way. Just keep an eye on things. Make sure nothing goes bad."

"Hurt? Hurt, I'm fucking thirty-one, Vinnie. I'm a fucking grown man."

"Joe wanted to be sure," Vinnie said.

Gerry's voice was shaking. "Stay the fuck away from me, Vinnie. You and him both, stay the fuck out of my life, you unnerstand? I don't need you. I was handling this, for crissake. I don't need you fucking wet-nursing me. I can handle it. I can handle any fucking thing. Stay the fuck away from me . . ."

His voice broke. He got up suddenly and pushed past Vinnie and went out the front door. Vinnie watched him go. He shook his head slowly. Then he turned and in a gesture that included all three bodyguards he jerked his head at the door. They went out after Gerry. Rocco stayed behind the bar.

Hawk remained motionless and silent at the back of the room.

Vinnie walked over and sat on a barstool next to me.

"You want some coffee?" he said to me.

"Sure," I said.

"Hawk?"

"Un huh."

"Rocco, give us three coffees," Vinnie said.

Rocco poured and served, bringing a mug back to Hawk, who accepted it silently. When he got through, Vinnie said, "Leave the pot, Rock, and go on out in the kitchen for a while."

Rocco put the coffeepot on the bar where Vinnie could reach it and went through the swinging doors. Vinnie leaned his elbows back on the bar.

"I thought we was going to cooperate on this thing," Vinnie said.

"I don't remember anything about not asking Gerry questions."

"Kid's a loose cannon, Spenser. You know that. Look what almost happened."

"That's why I badgered him," I said. "I know he's excitable, I thought something might pop out."

"Two barrels full of size-four shot were about to pop out in your face," Vinnie said.

"If he got the shot off," I said.

"Sure, sure," Vinnie said. "I know you're good." He nodded toward Hawk. "And I know he's good. But scattering fucking protoplasm around Rocco's isn't going to do anything for any of us."

I shrugged. "I probably wouldn't push him so hard if I had it to do over," I said.

Vinnie nodded. "You got to stay away from Gerry," he said. "Joe insists on it."

"Can't promise anything, Vinnie. Except that I won't harass him for fun."

"I insist too," Vinnie said.

"I know."

"This is about you too, Hawk," Vinnie said.

"I sort of guessed that, Vinnie."

"We still got some room here," Vinnie said. "But not very much. Joe's going to want to talk with you."

"Sure," I said. "How about Monday morning?"

"Come to the office about ten. Joe don't get in as early as he used to."

"Fine," I said and put the coffee cup down on the bar.

"I'll walk out with you," Vinnie said. "You never know about Gerry."

17

Lenox is two hours west from Boston on the Mass Pike. Paul and I rode out in the afternoon with Pearl leaning against the backseat, staring out the side window, alert as always for any sign of the elusive Burger King.

It doesn't take long on the Mass Pike to get away from the city and into what Massachusetts probably looked like in Squanto's day. Subtract a few houses here and there that back up to the turnpike west of Framingham, cancel out an occasional Roy Rogers or food & fuel stops, and the landscape is mostly low hills and woods, punctuated often enough by bodies of water that looked very brisk under the blue autumn sky. The hilliness allowed for some variety to the trip, allowing as it did for mild scenic vistas as the highway crested one low rise and you could see it curving gently up another hill a mile and a half ahead. It wasn't Arcadia, but it wasn't the New Jersey Turnpike either.

"She probably never should have had a kid," Paul said to me near Grafton.

"Ever?" I said.

He shrugged. "Who knows ever?" he said. "But she wasn't ready for one when I was born."

106

"How old was she?"

"Twenty. She got pregnant when she was nineteen and she married my father to have me. She was going to enter her junior year in college."

"But she didn't," I said. "Because she had to stay home with the baby."

"Yeah. She went down to Furman, my father played football there."

"I know," I said.

"And they lived in—what did they call them then? The on-campus housing?"

"Probably still called them Vets Apartments then," I said.

"Yes," Paul said. "That's right. When I was a little kid I used to think it meant vet as in veterinarian, and I couldn't figure out why they called it that."

In the backseat Pearl made a loud sigh and turned around once and resettled at the opposite window. I put my hand back and she gave it a lick.

"I was always afraid she'd leave me," Paul said. "As long ago as I can remember, I was afraid she'd just run away and leave me and I'd have to go to the home for little wanderers."

"Your father?" I said.

"He barely counts," Paul said. "It's like he wasn't there. My childhood memories are almost empty of him."

"What are they full of?" I said.

There wasn't much travel midday, midweek, going west. I was doing seventy in the right-hand lane on the theory that cops always look for speeders in the passing lane. A trucker going eastbound flashed his headlights at me and I slowed as I crested the next hill. There was a two-tone blue state police cruiser parked sideways on the median strip with a radar gun. I cruised serenely past him at about fifty-seven.

"Fear," Paul said. "Fear of being left. I was thin and whiny and had colds all the time and I used to cling to my mother like a cold sore. She couldn't stand it. She'd try to get me away from her so she could breathe and of course the more she tried the more I clung."

I nodded. I could hear the therapist's voice in Paul's, and behind the calm exposition of past events, the pain and lingering fear that engendered the pain. I wished Susan had come with us.

"Hard on both of you," I said.

"Sometimes she would actually hide under the bed," Paul said. "But I'd find her. She could run, but she couldn't hide."

"Too bad your father wasn't around," I said. "Be easier if you'd had more than one person bringing you up."

"He couldn't stand either one of us," Paul said. "Maybe at first he could, or did, or thought he ought to. I think my mother and he actually loved each other, whatever the hell that quite means. But they shouldn't have got married. They just . . ." Paul seemed wordless. He shook his head, put his hands up in a gesture of bafflement. "They just shouldn't have gotten married . . ." He stared straight ahead for a moment. Pearl leaned forward and snuffled at the back of his neck, and he put his hand up absently to pat her muzzle. "Or had me," he said.

"But they did," I said.

"But they did."

18

The Tailored Lady was a boutique off Church Street in downtown Lenox. It was in a sort of shopping center, where private houses had been converted to stores in which you could buy turquoise jewelry and Icelandic sweaters. The woman who ran it wore a blue blazer over a green turtleneck sweater.

She was very polite, but she couldn't tell us anything at all.

"I'm sorry," she said, "that I can't be more helpful. I could find my copy of the American Express receipt, but it would merely duplicate what you have."

"You don't remember if she was with anyone?" Paul said.

She smiled and shook her head. Matching the sweater and blazer was a Black Watch plaid skirt. Her blonde hair was caught back and tied with a little Black Watch ribbon.

"There are so many tourists," she said. "It's the start of the foliage season, and"—she smiled as if she were saying something daring—"the fall getaway time. A lot of women come in for lingerie." She paused as if weighing the propriety of what she said. "Usually there are men with them." She glanced demurely down at her Cobbie Cuddlers shoes.

"Where do they usually stay?" I said.

"Oh, there are so many places. It depends on price, I should think. There's a tourist information booth across the way that could probably give you a list."

She was looking straight at me and I realized she was appraising me. I grinned at her. The grin I used before Susan, the one where women slipped their house keys in my coat pocket as soon as I'd used it. I saw something show through for a moment in her face, passing over it the way the shadow of a cloud moves quickly across a field. And I knew that the Talbot's outfit was a disguise. And I saw the assertive body suddenly, inside the disguise. Then the look was gone again. But I knew I'd seen it, and she knew I'd seen it. It was my move. I smiled again, a modulated version of the killer grin, and said, "Thanks very much. Sorry to bother you."

And she said, "You're welcome." She was wearing an ornate wedding band with diamond chips set in it. But I knew that would not have been an issue. As Paul and I turned and went out of the store toward the tourist information center, I looked back once at the now apparent body that seemed so much realer than its inessential camouflage, and took a deep breath. *The price of monogamy.*

Across the way, a plump woman in a flowered purple dress gave us a printed list of area hotels and bed and breakfast accommodations. There were eighty-seven of them.

"Of course we only cover the immediate Lenox area," she said. "People come from all over the Berkshires and eastern New York State to shop. So your friends might very well be staying in Pittsfield or Williamstown or Albany, New York, even Saratoga."

"How encouraging," I said.

We took the listing, got a road map out of the car, and took both to a restaurant specializing in cheesecake. Paul had a chicken salad on light rye. I ordered a turkey on whole wheat with mustard. And another one plain to go. He had a Coke. I abandoned any hint of prudence and had coffee.

Neither of us had cheesecake.

"How we going to do this?" Paul said.

I drank some coffee. Not as much fun as the woman in the preppie disguise would have been. But better than nothing.

"Say your mother's with Beaumont. Which isn't a bad bet, since no one can find him either, and some good people are looking." I took a bite of the turkey sandwich. The menu had advertised fresh turkey. It seemed to be fresh from the turkey roll. It wasn't particularly good, but that was no reason not to eat it. "That being the case, if they are out here, and he gets a hint that someone's looking for him, they'll be gone ten minutes later. If he's in trouble with Broz he has reason to run."

I had another bite, another draught of coffee.

"So we can't just start calling places up," Paul said, "because somebody might tell him."

"Well, maybe if you called and asked for your mother," I said.

"What if he answers?" Paul said.

The waitress came past with coffee and refilled my cup. I rewarded her with a dazzling smile. She didn't notice.

"Say who you are. Ask for your mother."

"And if he hangs up?"

"We hotfoot it over there and try to get them before they leave."

"And if I get her?" Paul said.

"Tell her the deal," I said. "You're worried about her. You want to see her."

"And what if she hides under the bed?"

"I don't know what to do about that," I said.

"Why not get the police to help?"

I shook my head.

"Too delicate," I said. "The Lenox cops may be the ultimate police machine for all I know. But small-town police forces often aren't, and I'm afraid if they start looking for Richie and your mother that they'll spook them for sure." I put a second spoonful of sugar in my coffee. "Besides," I said, "they haven't done anything illegal that we know, but, if the cops get in it, and they have . . ."

"Yes," Paul said. "I understand. We've got to protect my mother in this."

I finished my sandwich, and ate the chips that came with it, and the sour pickle. I drank some coffee. The pickle made the coffee taste metallic.

"What if they are registered under another name?" Paul said.

"That's harder than everyone thinks it is," I said. "Unless you've got a lot of cash so that you needn't use a credit card, and you register someplace that doesn't require an identification. Most places do. Of course Beaumont may have credit cards and ID in another name. He sounds like the kind of guy that might."

"And if he does, and they use another name?"

"Then we won't find them this way," I said. "We'll find them another way."

"Well," Paul said, and his face seemed tight, and color-less, "it's not much of a plan but it's better than any that I've got."

I nodded. The waitress brought the check. I paid. We got up and went out to the car where I gave Pearl the plain turkey sandwich, and when she was through eating it I got some bottled water and a plastic dish out of the trunk and gave her a drink. Then Paul and I walked her on the leash around Lenox for about a half hour until she'd accomplished everything one would hope for, then we got back in the car and began looking for a motel that took dogs.

19

The Motel Thirty in Lee had no objection to Pearl. They also would have had no objection to the Creature From the Black Lagoon—or Madonna. We sat in a room with pink wallpaper on beds that had pink chenille bedspreads. Each of the beds would vibrate for five minutes if you put two quarters in a slot. Pearl circled the room carefully, went into the bathroom, drank noisily from the toilet bowl, came back out, selected one of the beds, hopped up, turned around three times, and lay down on it. Paul started calling.

It took three hours to call everyone on the list. No one had anyone named Rich Beaumont or Patty Giacomin registered. After the last call, Paul hung up the phone very carefully, and got up and walked to the window and looked out at the blacktop parking lot. He was perfectly still. His shoulders were hunched in angular pain, and for a moment I saw the fifteen-year-old kid I'd originally met, deadened with defeat, paralyzed with desperation.

"We'll find her," I said.

Paul nodded, and continued to stare down at the parking lot.

114

Pearl was quiet on the bed. Her head resting on her forepaws, her eyes on me, moving as I moved. She always watched me.

"When I was small," Paul said, "and my father was at work, and there was just me and her in the house, I remember I used to scheme to get her attention, not just to be nice, but to be responsible. I wanted her to be a mother. I'd be in my room and I'd spill something and I'd think, 'Okay, now she'll have to come in here and do something.' "

"Like an adult," I said.

Paul's back still had a quality of asymmetric tension to it as he spoke.

"Yeah."

"An adult could be trusted," I said.

"Yeah."

"An adult wouldn't leave you."

Without turning, Paul nodded. He put his hands in his pants pockets and leaned his forehead against the windowpane.

"Like she has again," I said.

The light outside the window was getting gray, and I could hear the wind picking up. Pearl looked uneasy, and her eyes followed me in even small movements.

"I been shrunk so much my skin's about to pucker," Paul said. "I know what's happening to me. I know why I feel like I do, and now I need to come to terms with it. But it still hurts just as if I didn't understand it."

"And when we find her?" I said.

The reminiscent shrug again.

"Getting past that takes more than understanding," I said.

115

"Yeah?" Paul said. "How about heavy drugs?"

"Always an option," I said.

A few drops of rain splattered heavily against the window. Pearl's ears went up and she stared at the window, then glanced quickly toward me. I put my hand on her shoulder and left it there. Outside it had gotten quite dark.

"You mean *will,* don't you?" Paul said.

"Yeah."

"You mean self-control."

"Yeah."

Paul turned slowly away from the window and looked at me seriously. His hands were still in his pockets. Behind him the fat raindrops were spattering more often against the glass, and the wind was rattling the window and skittering leaves across the blacktop in the parking lot among the economy cars and trucks with hunting caps on them.

"Heavy drugs would be easier," he said.

"I know," I said.

Outside, the storm came with a rush, driven by wind and slashed by lightning. It chattered against the window, and when the thunder followed, Pearl sat bolt upright and leaned against me and swallowed hard.

We were quiet inside the cheap motel room listening to the storm in the gathering darkness.

20

Joe was aging. He still carried himself with the theatricality he'd always had, as if there were an audience watching his every move, and he was playing to it. But he had gotten smaller, and his cheekbones had become more prominent, and his hair had thinned, though most of it was still black.

We were sitting in his office thirty-five floors up at the lower end of State Street. Behind Broz, through the rain-blurred picture window that covered that whole wall, I could see the harbor. The rain that had started yesterday in Lenox had followed us back, and had been slanting in on Boston uninterrupted for nearly twenty hours.

Joe was wearing a black suit with a matching vest. His shirt was white with cutaway collar, and he wore a gray and white striped tie with a big Windsor knot. Along the left wall was a full bar, complete with brass rail. Leaning against the bar with his elbows resting was Vinnie Morris.

"Usually," Joe was saying, "you are in the way, and it surprises me to this fucking moment that I haven't had someone hack you."

He had a deep phony voice, like the guys that call up

and give you a recorded sales pitch on the phone. He spoke as if diction were hard for him and he had to be careful not to speak badly.

"Everyone makes mistakes," I said.

"And every time I talk to you and listen to your smart mouth it surprises me more." He leaned back in his high-backed blue leather chair and clasped his hands behind his head. "This time we might have a common interest."

"I'd hate to think so," I said.

"Spenser," Vinnie Morris said from the bar, "we're trying to work something out. Whyn't you button it up a little bit."

"We could take a different approach," Joe said.

"Like Gerry did," I said.

"Gerry's got a temper," Joe said. "Who worth his salt don't have a temper? Huh? Tell me that. Guy's going to inherit this." Joe made an inclusive motion with his right hand. "Guy's got to have some pepper. Right, Vinnie?"

"Like you, Joe."

"That's right. I always had the fucking pepper. People knew it. Kept them in line. They knew I wouldn't back off. And they know Gerry's a piece of the same work."

Joe had unlaced his hands from behind his head and placed them flat on the desk where he was leaning over them, looking at me hard when he talked—a picture of intensity. But there was nothing there. It was a performance. Broz didn't believe it anymore. Vinnie and I never had.

Joe was silent for a minute, leaning forward over his desk, staring at me. I had the feeling he might have forgotten what he was saying.

"So what do you want to talk about?" I said.

Joe frowned at me.

"You want to say what the problem is with Gerry and Rich Beaumont?" Vinnie said to Joe.

"He wearing a wire?" Joe said.

"No, Joe."

"You checked him before?"

"Like always, Joe. Every body, every time."

"Good," Joe said. "Good."

We were quiet for a moment.

"Richie Beaumont," Vinnie said.

"Yeah. Richie." Joe shifted a little in his chair so I could see his profile against the rain-translucent picture window. "Him and Gerry were associated in a deal we had going."

"What kind of deal?" I said.

Joe raised the fingers of his left hand maybe two inches. "A deal. We have a lot of deals going."

"And Gerry's involved in all of them," I said.

Joe's shoulders shrugged. The movement was minimal, maybe a half an inch.

"He's my son," Joe said.

"So what makes this deal special?" I said.

Joe shrugged again. His shoulders hunched higher this time.

"Nothing special, just another deal we were doing."

I looked at Vinnie. He shook his head. I sat still and waited.

"Gerry's my only kid," Joe said.

I nodded. He was silent. On the window the rain twisted into thick little braids of water in places.

"I'm seventy-one."

I nodded some more.

119

"Like anybody coming into a business, he needs some room. Some room to make mistakes, unnerstand? Some chance to learn from the mistakes. How we all . . ." Joe made a little vague circle with his right hand. "How we all learned, got to be men. You and me, Spenser, we're men. You know? Vinnie too. We know how men do things. Because we learned. We made our mistakes and we survived them and we . . ." He made the gesture again with his right hand. "We fucking learned is all."

"Gerry made a mistake," I said.

"Sure," Joe said. "Sure he did. Everybody does when they're starting out. You can tell them, and tell them. But it's not the same, they got to do it themselves, and fuck it up. Like we did."

"Sure," I said.

Out across the harbor I could see a DC 10 angling down out of the overcast, slanting in through the rain toward Logan Airport. Joe was looking down at his hands spread on the desk top. Then he looked up at me, and for a moment the staginess was gone. For a moment there seemed to be something like recognition in his face and his eyes were, briefly, the eyes of an old man, tired, with time running down.

"We gotta let Gerry straighten this out himself," he said.

"So he can learn?"

"So he can feel like one of us, Spenser. So he can be a fucking man."

Broz got up suddenly and turned and stared out the picture window at the rain coming down over the harbor. To my left Vinnie was motionless. In the stillness I could hear the sound the rain made as it sluiced down the window, barely two inches from Broz's face.

"I don't care much about what Gerry becomes, Joe. I'm worried about the kid I know."

"The Giacomin kid." Joe didn't turn around.

"Yeah. He wants to find his mother. I told him we'd find her. We figure she's with Beaumont."

"Vinnie says you been with that kid a long time."

"Un huh."

Joe looked out at the rain some more.

"Tell him about the deal, Vinnie," Joe said. "And make me a drink. You want a drink, Spenser?"

"Sure," I said.

Vinnie moved behind the bar.

"What'll it be?" he said.

"Scotch and soda," I said. "Tall glass. Lot of ice."

Vinnie began to assemble the drinks.

"You know the kind of work we do," Vinnie said. "It requires some give and take with the law, you know?"

I said I knew.

"We make some gifts to people in Vice, to people on the OCU, maybe a captain in Command Staff, maybe an intelligence guy out at Ten Ten."

Vinnie had a Campari and soda mixed and brought it around the bar to Broz. Joe took it without turning from the window. He took a swallow and continued to stare at the rain while he held the glass.

"Some of these are standup guys, still do the job, bust the freaks, take out the street punks, but they give us a little edge. They treat us right, we treat them right. Some mutual respect. We got some good cops we do business with."

Vinnie was back behind the bar. He started putting my scotch and soda together while he talked. His voice was quiet in the big formal room.

"Well, Joe has this, whaddya call it, this network in place for a while. He builds it slow, careful, for a long time. Does business with guys we can trust, our kind of people, steady guys, you know? Not flighty, you might say."

He put the glass up on the bar and I stood and walked across the room and took it and went and sat back down. Vinnie started making himself a drink. Joe's back was perfectly still as he stared out the window. If he heard Vinnie talking he didn't show it. He stared at the rain as if he'd never see it again.

"Well, Joe's interested in Gerry learning all of the business, so he puts Gerry in charge of overseeing that part of things, paying out; and Gerry decides it should be changed a little."

Vinnie had a thick lowball glass of bourbon over ice. He took a taste as he walked around the bar, and leaned on it. He nodded his head slightly, approving of the bourbon. He glanced over at Joe's silent motionless back.

"Gerry started buying up cops like they were made in Hong Kong. He's paying off people at school crossings, you know. And he's got this guy Rich Beaumont as his bagman. Pretty soon Gerry's got a payroll, looks like the welfare list, makes us like the third-biggest employer in the state. And he's not choosy. Anybody he can bribe, he bribes. Joe hears about it first because one of our guys hears one of Gerry's guys bragging about it. About how he's got Gerry shoving money up his nose, and the guy's laughing. The guy can't do him any good. He's like in Community Relations and Gerry thinks he's still in Vice, and the guy's laughing at us."

"And talking," I said.

Vinnie looked at the bourbon in his glass for a long

moment. He stuck one finger in and moved the ice around a little and took the finger out and sucked off the bourbon, and ran the back of his hand across his lips.

"And talking," Vinnie said. He took another swallow of bourbon. I drank some scotch.

From the window Joe said, "Vinnie," and held his hand out with the empty glass in it. Vinnie walked over and took it and brought it back and made another one.

"So I talked with Joe about it," Vinnie said. "And we decided we'd have to talk with Gerry about it, only by the time we did get to talk with him . . ."

Vinnie walked across the room with the fresh Campari and soda and put it in Joe's hand. Then he returned to the bar and gazed for a moment at Joe's back. He took in some bourbon. Then he looked straight at me.

". . . Beaumont had taken off with a bagful of our money."

"How much?" I said.

Vinnie shook his head. "You don't need to know."

"No," I said, "I don't. But I need to know if it was enough."

"It was enough," Vinnie said. "He was skimming what he paid out and then, lately, he wasn't paying anybody—and mostly it was okay because the people he was supposed to be paying couldn't do us anything anyway."

"More than a million?" I said.

"Don't matter," Vinnie said.

"Matters when I look for him," I said. "Where I look depends on what he can afford."

"Okay, more than a million. He can afford pretty much anything he wants. But that ain't the point. The point is you can't stay in business and let a chipmunk like Richie

Beaumont take your money and give you the finger. He can't be allowed to get away with it."

"I understand that," I said. "I got no problem with that."

We were all quiet then, the three of us, sipping our drinks at 11:30 in the morning, while it rained outside.

From the window Joe said, "You gotta stay out of Gerry's way, Spenser. He's got to find Beaumont himself. He's got to get the money back. He's got to put Beaumont down. He don't do that, what is he? What kind of man is he to run this thing we got? What do they think of him? What do I think of him?"

Joe's voice had none of the audition-booth resonance now; it was hoarse. "What the fuck does he think of himself?"

"We got a problem," I said. "I don't say it can't be resolved, but it's a problem."

"We got nothing against the broad," Vinnie said.

"Sure," I said. "But what if she's with him when Gerry finds him, and he puts up a fight and Gerry has to kill him and she sees it? Or what if he's told her all about his deal with Gerry?"

"We guarantee her safety?" Joe said softly.

"You can't," I said.

"You wouldn't take my word on it?" Joe said. "Vinnie's word?"

"I'd take Vinnie's word, but not Gerry's."

"Or mine?"

I shrugged.

"We can't guarantee it, Joe," Vinnie said. His voice was flat, very careful.

Joe nodded slowly.

124

"You got a suggestion?" he said to me.

"I'll do the best I can, Joe. I don't like you but he's your kid. I find Beaumont, I'll leave him in place and take the woman. I won't hold Beaumont for Gerry, and I won't tell Gerry where he is, but I'll leave him out there for Gerry to hunt."

"You find him you give him to Vinnie," Broz said.

"And Vinnie will put him where Gerry can find him and Gerry will think he won."

Joe shrugged. I looked at Vinnie. Vinnie was staring past us both, looking at the harbor. There was no expression on his face.

"No," I said. "I won't give Beaumont to Vinnie."

Joe sighed slowly.

"There's an option we ain't spoken of yet," he said. He was tired; the *ain't* had crept in past his self-consciousness. "We could whack you."

"Maybe you could whack me," I said. "It's been tried. But where would that get you? It'll attract the attention of people you'd rather not attract. A lot of people know what I'm working on."

"Hawk," Vinnie said.

"For one," I said. "And there'd be a homicide investigation."

"Quirk," Vinnie said, as if he were counting off a list.

"So you trade me for them," I said, "maybe some others."

My drink was gone. I didn't want another one. The room was full of harshness and pain and a bitterness that had been distilled by silence. I wanted to get out of there.

"It's my kid, Spenser," Broz said. He sounded as if his throat were closing.

125

"I'm in sort of the same position, Joe."

"He's got to get some respect," Broz said.

I didn't say anything. Gerry wasn't going to get respect. He couldn't earn it and Joe couldn't earn it for him. Joe was silent, his hands folded, looking at his thumbs. He seemed to have gone somewhere.

After a while Vinnie Morris said, "Okay, Spenser. That's it. We'll talk to you later."

I stood. Broz didn't look up. I turned and walked toward the door across the big office. Vinnie walked with me.

At the door I said to Vinnie, "If Gerry gets in my way I will walk over him."

"I know," Vinnie said. He looked back at Joe Broz. "But if you do, you know who Joe will send."

I nodded. I turned back and looked at Joe.

"Tough being the boss's son," I said.

Joe didn't answer. Vinnie held the door open. And I went out.

21

Pearl didn't like the rain. She hung back when Susan and I took an after-dinner stroll, even when Susan pulled on her leash. And when we prevailed through superior strength, she kept turning and looking up at me, and pausing to jump up and put her forepaws on my chest and look at me as if to question my sanity.

"I heard that if you step on their back paws when they jump up like that, they learn not to," Susan said.

"Shhh," I said. "She'll hear you."

Susan had a big blue and white striped umbrella and she carried it so that it protected her and Pearl from the rain. Pearl didn't quite get it, and kept drifting out from under its protection and getting splattered and turning to look at me. I had on my leather trench coat and the replica Boston Braves hat that Susan had ordered for me through the catalogue from Manny's Baseball Land. It was black with a red visor and a red button. There was a white **B** on it and when I wore it I looked very much like Nanny Fernandez.

"What will you do?" Susan said.

"I'll try to extract Patty Giacomin from the puzzle and leave the rest of it intact."

"And you won't warn Rich?"

"No need to warn him. He knows he's in trouble."

"But you won't try to save him?"

"No."

"Isn't that a little flinty?" Susan said.

"Yes."

"Officially, here in Cambridge," Susan said, "we're supposed to value all life."

"That's the offical view here in Cambridge of people who will never have to act on it," I said.

"That is true of most of the official views here in Cambridge," Susan said.

"My business is with Patty—Paul really. Rich Beaumont had to know what he was getting himself into—and besides I seem to feel a little sorry for Joe."

Pearl had wedged herself between my legs and Susan's, managing to stay mostly under her part of Susan's umbrella, and while she didn't seem happy, she was resigned. We turned the corner off Linnaean Street and walked along Mass Avenue toward Harvard Square.

"You are the oddest combination," Susan said.

"Physical beauty matched with deep humility?"

"Aside from that," Susan said. "Except maybe for Hawk, you look at the world with fewer illusions than anyone I have ever known. And yet you are as sentimental as you would be if the world were pretty-pretty."

"Which it isn't," I said.

"You cook a good chicken too," Susan said.

"Takes a tough man," I said, "to make a tender chicken."

"How come you cook so well?"

"It's a gift," I said.

"One not, apparently, bestowed on me."

"You do nice cornflakes," I said.

"Did you always cook?" she said.

Pearl darted out from under the umbrella long enough to snuffle the possible spoor of a fried chicken wing, near a trash barrel, then remembered the rain and ducked back in against my leg.

"Since I was small," I said.

As we passed Changsho Restaurant, Pearl's head went down and her ears pricked and her body elongated. She had found the lair of the chicken wings she'd been tracking earlier.

"Remember," I said, "there were no women. Just my father, my uncles, and me. So all the chores were done by men. There was no woman's work. There were no rules about what was woman's work. In our house all work was man's work. So I made beds and dusted and did laundry, and so did my father, and my uncles. And they took turns cooking."

We were past Changsho, Pearl looked back over her shoulder at it, but she kept pace with us and the protective umbrella. There was enough neon in this part of Mass Avenue so that the wet rain made it look pretty, reflecting the colors and fusing them on the wet pavement.

"I started when I was old enough to come home from school alone. I'd be hungry, so I'd make myself something to eat. First it was leftovers—stew, baked beans, meat loaf, whatever. And I'd heat them up. Then I graduated to cooking myself a hamburg, or making a club sandwich, and one day I wanted pie and there wasn't any so I made one."

"And the rest is history," Susan said.

A big MBTA bus pulled up at the stop beside us, the water streaming off its yellow flanks, the big wipers sweeping confidently back and forth across the broad windshield.

"Well, not entirely," I said. "The pie was edible, but a little odd. I didn't like to roll out the crust, so I just pressed overlapping scraps of dough into the bottom of the pie plate until I got a bottom crust."

"And the top crust?"

"Same thing."

The pneumatic doors of the bus closed with that soft, firm sound that they make and the bus ground into gear and plowed off through the rain.

"My father came home and had some and said it was pretty good and I should start sharing in the cooking. So I did."

"So all of you cooked?"

"Yeah, but no one was proprietary about it. It wasn't anyone's accomplishment, it was a way to get food in the proper condition to eat."

"Your father sounds as if he were comfortable with his ego," Susan said.

"He never felt the need to compete with me," I said. "He was always very willing for me to grow up."

Pearl had located a discarded morsel of chewing gum on the pavement and was mouthing it vigorously. Apparently she found it unrewarding, because after a minute of ruminative mouthing she opened her jaws and let it drop out.

"There's something she won't eat," Susan said.

"I would have said there wasn't," I said.

130

We passed the corner of Shepard Street. Across Mass Avenue, on the corner of Wendell Street, the motel had changed names again.

"I got to shop some too," I said, "though mostly for things like milk and sugar. My father and my uncles had a vegetable garden they kept, and they all hunted, so there was lots of game. My father liked to come home after ten, twelve hours of carpentering and work in his garden. My uncles didn't care for the garden much, but they liked the fresh produce and they were too proud to take it without helping, so they'd be out there too. Took up most of the backyard. In the fall we'd put up a lot of it, and we'd smoke some game."

"Did you work in the garden?" Susan said.

"Sure."

"Do you miss it?"

"No," I said. "I always hated gardening."

"So when we retire you don't want to buy a little cottage and tend your roses?"

"While you're inside baking up some cookies," I said, "maybe brewing a pot of tea, or a batch of lemonade that you'd bring me in a pitcher."

"What a dreadful thought," Susan said.

"Yes," I said. "I prefer to think I can be the bouncer in a retirement home."

The Cambridge Common appeared through the shiny down-slanted rain. Pearl elongated a little when she sniffed it. There were always squirrels there, and Pearl had every intention of catching one.

"And you?" I said.

"When I retire?"

"Yeah."

131

Susan looked at the wet superstructure of the children's swing set for a moment as we crossed toward it.

"I think," she said, "that I shall remain young and beautiful forever."

We reached the Common and Pearl was now in low tension, leaning against the leash, her nose apparently pressed against the grass, sniffing.

"Well," I said, "you've got a hell of a start on it."

"Actually," she said, "I don't suppose either of us will retire. I'll practice therapy, and teach, and write some. You'll chase around rescuing maidens and slaying dragons, annoying all the right people."

"Someday I may not be the toughest kid on the block," I said.

She shook her head. "Someday you may not be the strongest," she said. "I suspect you'll always be the toughest."

"Good point," I said.

22

Paul and I were working out in the Harbor Health Club. Paul was doing pelvic tilt sit-ups. I could do some. But Paul seemed able to do fifty thousand of them and had the annoying habit of pausing to talk during various phases of the sit-up without any visible strain. He was doing it now.

"Maybe," he said, "we were out in Lenox asking the wrong questions of the wrong people."

I was doing concentration curls, with relatively light weight, and many reps. Paul had been slowly weaning me from the heavy weights. *It's the amount of work, not the amount of weight.*

"Almost by definition," I said, trying to sound easy as I curled the dumbbells. "Since what we did produced nothing."

"Well, I mean I know I'm a dancer and you're a detective, but . . ."

"Go ahead," I said. "If you've got a good idea, my ego can stand it—unless it's brilliant."

"It's not brilliant," Paul said. He curled down and up and down again, and began curling up on an angle to

133

involve the lateral obliques. "But if I had more than a million dollars in cash, and I were running away from the kind of people you've described, maybe I wouldn't stay in a hotel."

I finished the thirtieth curl and began to do hammer curls.

"Because you wouldn't be making a temporary departure," I said.

"That's right," Paul said. "You'd know you could never come back."

"So maybe you'd buy a place, or rent a place."

"Yes. I don't know what property costs, but if I had a million dollars . . ."

"More than a million," I said. "Yeah. You'd stay in a hotel if you were on your way somewhere. But if you were going to make it a permanent hideout, you'd want something more."

"Could you buy a place without proving your identity?" Paul said.

I put down the barbells. They were bright chrome. Everything was upscale at the Harbor Health Club except Henry Cimoli, who owned it. Henry hadn't changed much since he'd fought Willie Pep, except that the scar tissue had, with time, thickened around his eyes, so that now he always looked as if he were squinting into the sun.

"You'd have to give a name, but if you were paying cash, I don't think you'd have to prove it."

"So maybe we should go out there and talk to real estate people," Paul said.

"Yes," I said. "We should."

I finished my set of thirty hammers and went back to straight curls, concentrating on keeping my elbow still, using only the bicep.

"It's an excellent idea," I said.

Paul had gone into a hamstring stretch where he sat on the floor with his legs out straight and pressed his forehead against his kneecap.

"You'd have thought of it anyway," he said.

"Of course," I said. "Because I'm a professional detective, and you're just a performer."

"Certainly," Paul said.

We finished our workout, stretched, took some steam, showered, picked up Pearl from the club office where she had been keeping company with Henry, and strolled out into the fresh-washed fall morning feeling loose and strong with all our pores breathing.

In the car I said, "Is there a picture of your mother?"

"Should be, at the house."

"Okay, let's go out there and break in again and get it."

"No need to break and enter," Paul said. "While we were there last time I got a key. She always was losing hers, so she kept a spare one under the porch overhang. I took it when we left."

We went out Storrow Drive toward Route 2. A little past Mass General Hospital I spotted the tail. It was a maroon Chevy, and it was a very amateurish tail job. He kept fighting to stay right behind me, making himself noticeable as he cut in and cut off drivers to stay near my rear bumper. There was even horn blowing.

I said to Paul, "We are being followed by one of the worst followers in Boston."

Paul turned and looked out the back window.

"Maroon Chevy," I said.

"Right behind us?"

"Yeah. Probably someone from Gerry," I said. "Joe

would have someone better. If Vinnie Morris did it you wouldn't notice."

"Would you?"

"Yeah."

"What are we going to do?"

"We'll lose them," I said.

We continued out Storrow and onto Soldiers Field Road, past Harvard Stadium and across the Eliot Bridge by Mt. Auburn Hospital. In the athletic field near the stadium a number of Harvard women were playing field hockey. Their bare legs flashed under the short plaid skirts and their ankles were bulky with thick socks. The river as we crossed it was the color of strong tea, and a little choppy. A loon with his neck arched floated near the boat club. Behind us the maroon Chevy stayed close to our exhaust pipe. I could see two people in it. The guy driving was wearing sunglasses. Near the Cambridge-Belmont line, where Fresh Pond Parkway meets Alewife Brook Parkway there is a traffic circle. I went slowly around it with the Chevy behind me.

"Where we going?" Paul said.

"Ever see a dog circle a raccoon or some other animal it's got out in the open?"

"No."

I went all the way around the circle and started around again.

"They keep circling faster and faster until they get behind it," I said.

I held the car in a tight turn and put more pressure on the accelerator. The Chevy tried to stay tight, but he didn't know what was going on and I did. Also I cornered better than he did. He lost some ground. I pushed the car harder, it bucked a little against the sharpness of the turn but I held it in.

"I get it," Paul said.

"Quicker than the guy in the Chevy," I said. He was still chasing us around the circle. On the third loop I was behind him and as he started around again, I peeled off right and floored it out the Alewife Brook Parkway, past the shopping center, ran the light at Rindge Ave. by passing three cars on the inside, and headed up Rindge back into Cambridge. By the time I got to Mass Avenue he had lost us. I turned left and headed out toward Lexington through Arlington.

"Wily," Paul said.

"Float like a butterfly," I said. "Sting like a bee."

"Pearl's looking a little queasy," Paul said.

"Being a canine crime stopper," I said, "is not always pretty."

23

We started in Stockbridge, because Paul and I agreed that Stockbridge was where we'd buy a place if we were on the run. And it was easy. We left Pearl in the car with the windows part open diagonally across from the Red Lion Inn, walked across the street to the biggest real estate office on the main street in Stockbridge, and showed the picture of Patty Giacomin to a thick woman in a pair of green slacks and a pink turtleneck.

"Oh, I know her," the woman said. "That's Mrs. Richards. I just sold them a house."

The house she had sold them was about half a mile from town on Overlook Hill. They had purchased the house for cash under the name Mr. and Mrs. Beaumont Richards.

"Beaumont Richards," I said as we drove up the hill. "Who'd ever guess it was him?"

Paul was silent. His face seemed to have lost color, and he swallowed with difficulty. Pearl had her head forward between us, and Paul was absently scratching her ear.

I parked on the gravel at the edge of the roadway in front of the address we'd been given. It was a recently built Cape, with the unlandscaped raw look that newly built houses have. This one looked even rawer because it was isolated, set into the woods, away from any neighbors. The roadway that we parked on continued into the woods. As if, come spring, an optimistic builder would put up some more houses for spec. Running up behind the house were some wheel ruts which appeared to do service as a driveway. The ruts had probably been created by the builders' heavy equipment and would be smoothed out and re-sodded in spring. To the left the hill sloped down toward the town, and you could see the Red Lion Inn, which dominated the minimalist center. Behind the house the woods ran, as best I could tell, all the way to the Hudson River.

"How to do this?" I said.

"I think I should go in," Paul said.

"Yeah, except Beaumont is bound to be very nervous about callers," I said.

"I'm his paramour's son," Paul said. "That's got to count for something."

"He's scared," I said. "That counts for everything in most people, if they're scared enough."

"I have to do this," Paul said. "I can't have you bring me in to see her. I am a grown man. She has to see me that way. She has to accept that . . . that I matter."

He swallowed. He had the look of bottled tension that he'd had when I first met him.

I nodded. "I'll be here," I said.

Paul made an attempt at a smile, gave me a little thumbs-up gesture, and got out of the car. Pearl immediately came into the front seat and sat where Paul had sat.

I watched him walk up the curving flagstone pathway toward number 12. It had a colonial blue door. The siding was clapboard stained a maple tone. There were diamond panes in the windows. There was no lawn yet, but some-

139

one had put in a couple of evergreen shrubs on each side of the front door and a quiet breeze gently tossed the tips of their branches. I wished I could do this for him. It cost him so much and would cost me so little. But it would cost him much more if I did it for him. He stopped on the front steps and, after a moment, rang the doorbell.

The door opened and I could see Paul speak, and pause, and then go in. The door closed behind him. I waited. Pearl stiffened and shifted in the seat as a squirrel darted across the gravel road and into the yellowing woods that had yielded only slightly to the house. I rubbed her neck and watched the front door.

"Life is often very hard on kids, Pearl," I said.

Pearl's attention remained fixed on the squirrel.

There was no sound. And no movement beyond that which the breeze caused to stir in the forest. Beaumont had chosen a bad place to hide. It seemed remote but its remoteness increased his danger. He'd have been better off in a city among a million people. Out here you could fire off cannon and no one would hear.

Pearl's head shifted and her body stiffened. The front door opened and Patty Giacomin came down the front walk with a welcoming look on her face. She still looked good, very trim and neat, with her blonde hair and dark eyes. She was dressed in some kind of Lord & Taylor farmgirl outfit, long skirt over big boots, an ivory-colored, oversized, cable-knit sweater, and her hair caught back with a colorful headband.

I rolled the window down on the passenger side half-way so I could speak to her. Pearl, who was standing on all fours now in the front seat, thrust her head through the opening, her tail wagging.

140

"Well, hello, you beautiful thing," Patty said and put a hand out for Pearl to sniff. "And you, my friend," she said to me. "How can you sit out in the car like a stranger? Come in, meet Rich, see my new house. It's been too long."

I nodded and smiled. "Nice to see you, Patty," I said and got out of the driver's side. Pearl turned toward me and looked disappointed when I closed the door on her. I went around the car and Patty Giacomin gave me her cheek to kiss.

"Come on in," she said again. "And bring this lovely dog. I couldn't bear it if she had to sit out here all alone, while we're all up in the house visiting."

I opened the passenger door and Pearl jumped out and dashed around in front of the house with her nose to the ground until she found a spot where she could squat. Which she did. I stuck her leash in my hip pocket.

Patty took my hand as if we used to be lovers, and led me to the front door. Pearl joined us there, and when Patty opened it, pushed in ahead of us. Paul was in the living room with a guy that looked like a *People* magazine cover boy. The living room was what I expected it would be. Knotty pine paneling, big fieldstone fireplace. Beams, wooden furniture with colonial print upholstery, a braided rug on the floor.

"Rich," Patty said, "I'd like you to meet someone," and gestured me toward him like I was the ambassador from Peru. Rich put out his hand and I took it. He didn't seem very pleased.

"Coffee?" Patty said. "A drink? Paul, do you drink now?"

Paul said, "Yes, I do, but not right now, thanks."

141

I shook my head. Rich was leaning against the wall near the fireplace with his arms folded. He was probably my height, which made him 6' 1", sort of willowy without being thin. He had thick dark hair which he wore brushed straight back, and longish so that it curled over his ears. He had a mustache that was just as black, and a tuft of black hair showed at the vee of his shirt, which he wore with the top three buttons open. It was a lavender dress shirt. His jeans were stone washed and designer labeled, and his lizard skin cowboy boots were ivory colored and would have been a nice match to Patty's sweater. Except for the mustache his dark face was cleanshaven, with the shadow of a dark beard lurking. His nose was strong and straight. His eyes were dark and moved a lot. If you had told him he was the cat's ass he'd have given you no argument.

"Paul says he was worried about his mom," Patty said and dazzled me with her even smile. "And I want to thank you for looking out for him."

"I wasn't looking out for him," I said. "He does that himself. I was helping him look for you."

She smiled again just as if I'd told her that her hair was looking lovely.

"As you can see, I'm fine. Rich and I just wanted to"— she waved her arms a little—"elope."

Paul said, "Did you get married?"

Patty smiled even more beguilingly.

"Well, not exactly, if you mean all that foolishness with organ music and somebody saying a bunch of words. But we love each other and wanted to get away and be alone."

I was quiet. My size made Rich uncomfortable. I don't know how I knew that, but I knew it. There was something about how he looked at me and shifted a little on the wall. But it wasn't a total setback for him; he still managed to look contemptuous.

"And you didn't think you needed to tell me?" Paul said. "Where you were, or even that you were going?"

"Shame on you, young man," Patty said. "Using that tone with your mother."

I could see Paul lower his head a little and shake it as if a swarm of gnats were bothering him. I shut up.

"It's the tone that this calls for," Paul said. His voice was tight, but it was clear. "I am your son, your only child, I should know where you are. Not every minute, but if you are making any moves of substance you should tell me. Do you realize what we've been doing to try and find you?"

"Paul, honey, Rich and I needed to get away, not tell anyone, Rich was very clear about that. Weren't you, darling?"

I've never heard anyone call anyone *darling* without sounding like a fool, except Myrna Loy. Patty wasn't close.

"Your mother and I wanted a kind of a honeymoon," Rich said. He had a great voice. He sounded like William B. Williams. "You're a big boy, we figured she could go off for a bit without you."

"So you went away for a bit and bought a house?" Paul said. He wasn't going to flinch.

Rich shrugged. Patty looked a little confused. "Paulie," she said. "Paulie, did you come all the way here to argue with your mother? Do you care if I'm happy?"

Paul shook his head again and plowed ahead.

"For cash?" Paul said. "Under another name?"

"Jeez," Rich said. "You got some nosy kid here, Patty."

Patty's eyes were bigger than was possible. "No," she said. "No, no."

"Does my mother know what you're running away

143

from?" Paul said. There was a rasp in his voice now. I was perfectly still, near him, and a little behind. I looked at Rich Beaumont. But I said nothing. This was Paul's, not mine.

"Hey, kid, you got some kind of bad mouth," Beaumont said. "For crissake lighten up. We went off and didn't tell you. So let's not make a big fucking deal about it."

"Richard!" Patty said and put the back of her hand against her mouth.

"Do you know?" Paul said.

"Paulie, you stop this. I was glad to see you, but now you're spoiling everything."

"Ma," Paul said. He was leaning forward a little as he talked.

"Listen to me," he said. "Do you know who you're with? Do you know why he doesn't want anyone to know where he is? Do you know why he bought the house under another name? And where he got the money?"

They both spoke at once. Rich said, "Hey—"

And Patty said, "Damn you, Paul, I don't want to know! I'm happy, don't you understand that? I'm happy."

Everyone was quiet then for a moment until Paul said, "Yes, but you're not safe."

The silence rolled in as if from a far place and settled in the room. Everyone stood still, not knowing what to say. Except me. I knew what I should say, which was nothing. And I kept saying it.

Finally Patty looked at Rich, and he said, "Kid, you got no business coming in here and talking like that. And you wouldn't get away with it if you didn't have this Yahoo with you."

"That may be," Paul said, "but here he is."

The Yahoo smiled charmingly and said nothing. He was musing over the prospect of stuffing Rich up the chimney flue if the opportunity appeared. From the sofa where she had settled, Pearl yawned largely. Her jaws opened so wide when she yawned that it ended with a squeak which may have been her jaw hinge. I was never quite sure.

"Paul," Patty said. "Please. Don't do this. I've found someone. Rich cares about me. You don't know what being alone is like."

"The hell I don't," Paul said.

From where I stood I could look into the big round gilded Eagle mirror over the fireplace and see my car parked down the slope of the lawn-to-be.

"What did you mean about safe?" Patty said.

"Are you going to tell her?" Paul said to Rich. "Or am I?"

"I am," Beaumont said. "It's not as bad as it sounds, but I was in business with a guy who turned out to have mob connections, and I took some money he says belongs to him."

"And they want it back," Patty said.

Beaumont nodded.

"Well, just give it to them," Patty said.

Beaumont shook his head.

"Why not?" Patty said. "Tell them you're sorry and give them the money."

"And this house?" Beaumont said.

"Yes, certainly, sell it. Tell them you'll make good. You have some money."

"None I haven't stolen," Beaumont said. There was no scornfulness in his voice this time, nor self-regard. It was

145

the voice of someone noticing an ugly thing about himself.

"I don't care. Give it to them. We have each other, we
can start over, give them the money back."

Beaumont was silent. Paul looked at me.

"It's not that simple," I said. "They intend to kill him."

Patty put her hand to her mouth again in the same
gesture she'd used when Beaumont said *fuck*. Patty's re-
action range was limited.

"But if he gives the money back . . ." she said.

Beaumont was looking past her out the sliding doors at
the end of the living room, which opened out onto the
green and yellow woods. He didn't say anything.

"It's a matter of principle now," I said. "These particu-
lar people can't let him get away with it. They have to kill
him."

All of us were quiet.

Patty said, "Richard?"

Beaumont nodded.

"He's right," Beaumont said. "It's why we had to come
here and hide. It's why I couldn't let you tell anyone at all.
Not even your kid."

"Richard," she said, "we better go away then."

"We're all right here," Beaumont said. "No one knows
we're here." He looked at us. "Do they?"

"No," I said.

"No one followed you?"

"No."

"You're sure?"

"Yes."

"Richard, we can't stay here," Patty said. "They might
find you."

"How'd you find us?" Beaumont said.

"A charge purchase from Lenox," I said.

Beaumont looked at Patty. "I told you cash," he said. "No charges."

"What harm? It was for us, like our honeymoon. Just that one time is all, Richard. I didn't know."

"What harm? For Christ's sake, Patty, they found us." He tossed his chin at Paul and me. "What if it had been Gerry?"

"Who?"

Beaumont made a dismissive wave with his hand.

"Is Gerry the one you took the money from?"

"Yeah."

"Richard, let's go somewhere else."

Beaumont started to shake his head and then stopped and turned his gaze slowly toward Patty.

"Why?" he said.

"It's too close. They might find us."

"What's going on, Patty?" Beaumont said. "Why might they find us?"

Patty had both hands pressed against her mouth now. She shook her head soundlessly.

"Ma," Paul said, "if you know something you have to say, this is—" He didn't finish.

Patty kept shaking her head with her hands pressed against her mouth.

"You told somebody," Beaumont said. "Goddamn you, you told somebody."

With her head still down and her hands still pressed, she was able to squeeze out the word "Caitlin."

"Caitlin Martinelli? You told her?"

She nodded and took her hands away. "I was so excited," she said, "about buying our house . . ." She wanted to say more and she couldn't.

"Who told her brother," I said, "who told Joe."

Beaumont nodded and turned and went out of the room. He came back almost at once wearing one of those fleece-lined cattleman's jackets that you can buy in a catalogue and carrying a blue and red Nike gym bag with a shoulder strap.

"I'm out of here," he said. "If you want to come, Patty, come right now. No packing, just come."

As he turned toward her I could see that he had a white-handled automatic stuck in his belt.

Patty looked at Beaumont and then at Paul, and then at her living room with all its fresh-from-the-showroom-floor furniture.

"I . . ." she said and stopped. "I don't . . ."

"Patty, damn you, decide," Beaumont said, moving toward the back door.

In the big mirror over the fireplace I saw a dark blue Buick sedan pull up behind my car on the gravel roadway. Another car, a white Oldsmobile, pulled in right behind it.

"They're here," I said. "Beaumont, take Paul and Patty. Get the hell out of here. Paul, when you get safe, call Hawk."

Eight men got out of the cars. Four from each. One of them had a shotgun. I knelt by the front window and knocked a diamond pane out with the muzzle of the Browning.

Paul looked at me and then at his mother and didn't say a word. He took her arm and dragged her out through the sliders where Beaumont had already gone.

Outside somebody yelled, "Window to the left of the door!"

I thumbed back the hammer and shot the first guy up the walk in the middle of the chest. He went over backwards and fell on his back. The others dashed for cover behind the cars. Carefully I shot out the tires on each car. Two tires per car, so the spare wouldn't help. I'm a good shot, but I'm not Annie Oakley. It took six rounds. But it also served to pin them down since they didn't know I wasn't shooting at them. At the first gunshot Pearl sat straight upright, at the second round she bolted out through the still-open sliders. I opened my mouth to yell and closed it. It wouldn't do any good, a gun-shy dog will run no matter what, and she was probably better off in the woods than she was going to be in here pretty soon.

Everything was quiet for the moment. Beaumont must have kept his car stashed on the rutted track behind the house. I never heard it start up, never saw it leave. For all the outfit outside knew, I was Beaumont, still in the house.

I had six rounds left in the Browning, and no spare clip. I hadn't thought Stockbridge would require it. There were seven bad guys left. One of them was Gerry Broz. If I shot each of them with one bullet, I would still have Gerry to strangle. It didn't seem good odds. From behind the Buick there was movement and then my window shattered and the shotgun boomed. The odds weren't getting better. The shotgun fired again and I moved to another window in time to see two bad guys crouched low, running right, and two more doing the same thing in the opposite direction. They were going to close me in from all sides. Anyone would. I smashed another pane out and nailed one of the low-running bad guys with my eighth round, and rolled back against the wall as the glass billowed out of this window with the boom of the shotgun. Hard upon the shotgun was the chatter of some kind of small-bore automatic weapon. I had five rounds left and was badly outgunned. Pearl had the right idea. I crouched as low as I could and ran for the open patio door, my feet crunching on the scattered shards of window glass. I felt something slap my left leg and then I was through the door and into the woods. I was maybe thirty yards in before the automatic fire stopped behind me. Behind me there was silence again. And then more automatic fire. The gunfire ceased. All I could hear was the sounds of my own breathing, steady but deep, and the sound I made, moving as quietly as I could though the fall foliage, heading west. My left leg was starting to throb and I could feel the warmth where it was bleeding. I stopped and peeled off my jacket. I ripped the sleeves off my sweatshirt, put my jacket back on. I folded one sleeve into a pad and tied it in place over my jeans, using the other sleeve. It was a bulky bandage and unsightly, but it seemed to suppress the bleeding.

Behind me I heard a yell that was nearly screaming. I knew it was Gerry.

"Richie, you're a dead man! You hear me? We're coming, you motherfucker. We got a tracker, asshole, and we're right behind you."

And then I didn't hear anything.

24

As I moved into the woods it got thicker and the going got harder. There was still green on the trees, mixed with yellow, and the combination gave a soft dappled effect to the forest. I didn't feel soft and dappled. And as the afternoon dwindled it got darker. After about a mile I limped up a low swale and settled in behind a rock to take stock. Behind me the woods had thinned into some sort of meadow; maybe a fire, maybe a homestead, long since consumed by the slow fire of decay. Whatever it had been caused by, it made an open space where I could see anyone following me.

I was wearing New Balance running shoes, jeans, a blue sweatshirt, now sleeveless, and a leather jacket. I had five rounds in my gun, my car keys, a wristwatch, and Pearl's leash still stuck in my hip pocket. My leg was very sore and the pain pulsed steadily along it from hip to ankle. There was a Buck knife in my jacket pocket, and two packets of matches wrapped in foil to keep them dry. I always carried the gun, the keys, and the watch. The knife and the matches were for when I went west of the Charles River. The minute I noticed that I had no food, I started getting hungry. The sun was setting. That would be west. I could keep going until dark without getting turned around. I'd have to stop at night. The sun I could figure out. I couldn't read the stars to save my ass, which was not, in this case, a metaphor.

I needed a plan. First I had to figure out if Gerry and his troops really were after me. Or Richie, which is who they thought I was. If they weren't I could simply back-track to Stockbridge and wait for Pearl. But if they were behind me, between me and Stockbridge, and if any of them knew how to function in the woods, and if they really had a tracker, then I'd need to take the long way home.

The way to find that out was to sit here behind these rocks, while I still had some ammo, and see if they showed up. They'd leave somebody behind to clean up the shooting scene and call Vinnie Morris and get some new tires. Unless someone came by at the wrong time, or somebody had heard the shooting and called the cops, they'd be okay. They had no way to know that Beaumont had bailed out with Patty and Paul, and that, in a while, Hawk was going to be coming out looking for me.

It didn't figure for Gerry and his posse to blunder around in the woods for several days looking for me. Ordinarily I figured to outrun them even if they did. But my leg wasn't going to improve. And Gerry was crazy. I settled in to wait. The late sun was warm enough on my back, but above me and moving slowly westward was a mass of dark clouds. And as the evening crept in from the east with the clouds, I could feel the edge of cold that was going to come with darkness.

They could have a tracker. They could have picked up

a couple of shooters in Pittsfield. One of them could be a woodsman. Or Gerry could have made it up because he'd heard the word once on television.

The woods through which I'd edged my way, and the ones which stretched out behind me, were mostly hardwoods, oak and maple, with some birch clumps scattered among them, dark-ringed white trunks that gleamed among the drabber trees like hope in the midst of sorrow. Sprinkled among the hardwoods were evergreens—a lot of white pine, now and then a good-looking fir tree. The forest floor was a tangle of roots, and fallen trees, and creeping vines. Many of the vines were thorny and would not only trip, but clutch. There were chokecherry bushes, many of them with caterpillar tents stretched across the more comfortable crotches near the trunk. In a pinch, I knew you could eat chokecherries, though they were pretty sharp. You could eat acorns too.

The combination of rain clouds and evening fell darkly across the little open space in front of me. In the woods it would be quite dark. There was some wind. I had already zipped my jacket and turned up my collar. It left me out of options for the moment.

To my right I heard movement in the woods. Quietly I eased the hammer back on the Browning. The movement continued, and then Pearl emerged from the woods, her nose against the ground, her head moving from side to side, her tail erect; she came across the meadow walking very fast, and up the swale, and then raised her head and capered around the rock and began to turn tight circles. I tried to hug her but she was too excited. When she stopped the circles, she sniffed me all over at a great rate. When she sniffed the gun she shied away briefly, and I lowered it beside my thigh, out of sight. She sniffed with special attention at my wounded leg, smelling the blood.

"Nice to see you," I said. She sat intensely and looked at me with her tongue out.

"What are we going to do if I have to shoot again?" I said. "You'll bolt and where will you end up?"

She had no answer. Neither did I. But it was bothersome.

25

It was full dark now, no moon, and the rain had begun. Pearl hated the rain and kept looking at me to do something about it. She also had not been fed since morning and was looking at me to do something about that, too.

"You're supposed to be a goddamned hunting dog," I said. "Maybe you should go hunt up something to eat."

She had curled in against the rock, behind me, with her head resting on her rear feet. The leather jacket kept my upper body dry, but my legs were soaked, and my hair, and a trickle of rain was worming down my neck inside the jacket. The bandage felt tight against the wound in my thigh. The leg was swelling.

"It doesn't get much better than this, Pearl."

Pearl's eyes moved toward me when I spoke. The rest of her was motionless.

"We're going to have to find something better," I said. "If Gerry's out there. He won't be chasing me in the rain, at night."

I stood, and Pearl immediately uncurled and stood with me, pushing against my good leg. I started down the swale west toward the woods when I smelled something. I stopped, and with the wind coming from the east driving the rain, I breathed in carefully though my nose, my eyes closed, my head a little forward. What I smelled was woodsmoke. They were in the woods, east of me, and they had hunkered down for the night and gotten a fire going. It meant probably that whether he was a tracker or not, they had someone with them who knew his way in the woods. Gerry couldn't have started a fire in the Public Gardens.

"I could slide over there and pick some of them off," I said.

Pearl pricked her ears and wagged her tail. "But if I do you'll bolt again."

I gazed obliquely off toward the area east, where the wind was bringing the smoke from. I was trying to spot the light of the fire. There had been eight. I had dropped two. At least one guy would have had to stay behind to clean things up at Beaumont's. That meant five people probably. It would need a proper fire to service five people. "I could put on your leash," I said. "But that means dragging you through the woods and holding you while I shoot and you're bucking and struggling to run, and then ducking through the woods with you still on the leash and several gunnies chasing me. And I've only got one leg that's really usable." I was staring up, above the treeline, looking for the glow of the fire. And I found it, east and a little south, some distance away. How far was more than I could estimate. Where was Jungle Jim when you really needed him?

With them in the light and me in the dark, and taking time to aim, I could probably pick off two of them before they got under cover. That would improve the odds.

Maybe I could tie her here and pick her up on the way back. If I came back. If I could find this place, running, on one and a half legs, in the dark. I looked at the fire glow in the sky east of me, and looked at Pearl, and turned and began to walk west. Pearl came along, staying close in the cold rain.

Working slowly, bumping into bushes and tree limbs, tripping over things on the forest floor, hurting my leg, I moved west, away from Broz. The darkness was nearly impenetrable. We began to go uphill again. I couldn't see it; I could tell by the increased resistance as I walked. Pearl was directly behind me, letting me break trail. I was cold now, and wet, and tired from fighting through the heavy cover.

At the top of the rise I walked into a big tree that had fallen. I worked my way down toward the root ball and found what I had hoped, the uprooting had left a shallow declivity, with the root ball shielding it partially, so that it was relatively dry in there, close to the roots. Pearl and I went in. I scraped away some of the leaf cover until I found leaves that felt dry. I heaped the leaves against the root ball, crumpled a dollar bill from my wallet in among them, piled on some twigs, and carefully lit the bill. It caught and flickered and spread to the leaves. I hovered over it, shielding it from the wind and stray raindrops. When the twigs caught I had enough flame to cast a little light, and I could see more twigs, and bigger ones. Carefully I added them, and bigger sticks, until I had a committed fire. Then I went out into the ring of light that the fire cast and got real firewood in the form of fallen limbs. I piled these under the shelter of the root ball and added some judiciously until I had a big fire. I augmented the

157

shelter of the root ball with evergreen boughs that I cut and laid carefully in a crisscross pattern. Then I got in under and tried to be comfortable.

"They've got their own fire," I said. "They won't smell this one. Or see it." Pearl was in close to the root ball, near the fire. I could see the steam rise from her coat as she began to dry.

"Tomorrow we'll swing north toward the Mass Pike. Route 90 runs all the way from Boston to Seattle, we're bound to hit it."

I was so tired I couldn't hold my head up. I took the Browning out and held it in my right hand, and folded my left hand over it, and put my head back.

"Okay, Pearl," I said. "Stay alert for prowlers."

My eyes fell shut. I opened them once to look at the dog. She was asleep.

"Better hope for no prowlers," I said. The fire glimmered briskly, the rain fell steadily, and the darkness endured. My eyes fell closed again. And stayed closed. And I slept, though all night I was aware that my leg was throbbing.

26

What woke me was the sound of Pearl drinking water from a puddle which had formed at the other end of the root hole. It was daylight. Still raining. I felt very sore. My leg felt swollen and hot. The fire was out. I wasn't dry. And I was hungry. I scooped a little water out of the puddle with my cupped hand and drank. It was muddy tasting with a nose of pine needles. I looked at the sky.

"Sun would be nice," I said. "Be warmer. Be drier. Be able to tell directions a lot easier."

Pearl was sitting looking at me with the expectation of breakfast.

"Well, it's better than sitting in some quarantine pen in England, isn't it?"

The sky was lightest back where east should be. North was along the top of this slope we had climbed up in the night.

"We'll head out," I said. "And we'll keep an eye out for breakfast. Nature never failed the heart that loved her."

Every few yards I would stop and listen. If they found me they'd kill me. The fact that I wasn't Beaumont would mean nothing. Gerry was going to kill somebody, and if

159

it were me it would please him fine. Ahead of me the land
sloped down. The leg would slow me down more and
more until I got it cleaned out and healing. Which meant
I had better get out of the woods pretty quick or have a
plan for dealing with them when they caught up with me.
I wasn't going to outwalk them.

As the land continued to drop, I could see a gray glint
of water through the trees. I was feeling feverish now, and
turned my face up toward the rain to cool it. Pearl was a
little ahead of me. She seemed to have gotten used to the
rain. I don't think she liked it, but it didn't puzzle her
anymore, and she had stopped turning and looking at
every raindrop that hit her. Suddenly I saw her drop her
head low, her belly sucked up, her neck extended, and
then she charged, running like pointers do, using more of
their front feet than their rear. She swerved sharply right,
then back left, and I realized she had an animal in front
of her. It was a groundhog. She had it trapped in the open
away from its hole. It couldn't outrun her, and near the
edge of a pond it turned and crouched. Pearl swung half
around it as she came up on the groundhog and grabbed
him by the back of the neck. She gave one sharp shake
and broke its neck and dropped it and turned it over and
began to eat it, ripping open its belly and eating the vis-
cera.

My baby had given way for a moment to something
older and more fundamental. She wasn't cute while she
ate the groundhog.

Along the edge of the marsh I found some Jerusalem
artichokes, and uprooted one, cut off the potato-esque
tubers on the roots, peeled and ate it. It was like eating
a raw potato, but less tasty. Still it was nourishment, and

160

it beat chasing down a groundhog. I put a couple more of the tubers in my pocket for through-the-day snacking.

The pond looked like a glacial gouge that had slowly filled in over the millennia. Its surface was dappled with rain, and there were weeds, including Jerusalem artichokes, along the margin. I found an area where I could get at the water and knelt and drank some. It had the strong rank taste of vegetation. Carefully I took off the bloody bandage and washed it in the pond. I dropped my jeans. The wound was dark with crusted blood and the flesh around it was puffy and red. I found some kind of moss in among the rocks along the margin of the pond and wet it and mixed it with some mud and put it on the wound like a kind of poultice. Then I wrapped it with the wet sweatshirt sleeves to hold it in place and tied it again and pulled my pants back up, edging the trouser leg carefully over the mess of a bandage.

Pearl finished with the groundhog. I went over and looked at the carcass. It was about half devoured. I picked it up and put it inside my jacket. Pearl would be hungry again, and despite her initial success, I wasn't confident that she could live off the land. She jumped up to sniff where I had stashed the carcass and rested one big paw on my wounded leg. I yelped and she dropped to the ground and backed off a yard and sat down very quickly, looking at me with her ears pricked forward and her head canted.

"Come on," I said, and we moved north again.

I ate some chokecherries, which were quite biting, and I found some acorns which I cracked and chewed and swallowed despite the strong bitterness of the tannin in them. If I had had something to soak them in, and time,

161

I could have leached out the tannin. But I didn't, and if I had, how good are leached acorns anyway? Later on, as we moved through the heavy cover, I gnawed at some more of the Jerusalem artichoke root. Everything I ate tasted like tarantula juice, but I knew I had to eat, and this was the best I could find.

The drizzle was persistent. By noontime I was beginning to feel light-headed, and the pulsing in my leg was Wagnerian. I wasn't going to be able to walk for too much longer. We crossed a stream, and again I washed my wound and washed the bandages and tied them back in place. I paused and stood still, listening. I couldn't hear anything except the sound the rain made in the woods. The ground rose ahead of me and I went up it. Whenever I could I stayed on the high ground, where it was a little easier going than the hollows. I found a big old pine and climbed it clumsily; my left leg was feeling more and more useless. Except for the pain it was largely without feeling, as if the pulsing insulated from everything else. When I got as high as the tree could support me, I wedged myself into a crotch, with one arm wrapped around the trunk and waited and watched. Below me Pearl sat on the ground, looking up. The half-gnawed groundhog inside my jacket was beginning to ripen. My hair was wet and the water dripped onto my forehead and into my eyes. I was feverish, and hot, except that I was also cold, and the effort of climbing the tree had made me more than light-headed. I was dizzy.

I took in some air, and exhaled, and did that a couple of times, and concentrated on the woods behind me, where Pearl and I had come from. Maybe a mile back was a bare patch, a basalt outcropping of maybe thirty or forty yards. I focused on it. Pearl and I had crossed it maybe forty minutes ago, and if they were behind us they'd cross it too. Not only did my trail lead that way—if they really had somebody who could follow a trail—but anyone would head for it because it was much easier going, if only for a little ways.

The acorns and chokecherries and Jerusalem artichokes rolled unpleasantly around in my stomach. The drizzle had upgraded again to a steady rain. The smell of pitch and pine needle and wetness was very strong as I pressed against the tree. A double Glenfiddich on the rocks would have been helpful. Pearl whined a little, nervously, from the ground under the tree. I said "shhh" automatically, the way people do with dogs, even though dogs generally don't know what "shhh" means. In Pearl's case I was up so high, and shhh'd so weakly, that Pearl probably didn't hear it anyway.

And then I saw them. Mostly I had been hoping I wouldn't and I could concentrate on making it to the Mass Pike before my leg gave way. But they were there, in three groups. In front a big dark guy, with long black hair, wearing a red and black mackinaw. He was tracking—his head down, swiveling slowly back and forth.

"Son of a bitch," I said. My voice sounded hoarse and funny.

Behind him were three other men. I recognized Maishe from the restaurant in Beverly, and Anthony. The third guy wasn't anyone I knew. He carried a white sack in his left hand. And behind them, straggling, maybe ten yards back, was Gerry Broz. He was laboring.

The white sack was probably a pillowcase. He'd probably had the brains to grab it and fill it with whatever

163

foodstuffs he could find in Patty Giacomin's kitchen. He was smallish, and wiry looking, from where I was watching. And he looked country, like the tracker. Maishe had an Uzi, and Anthony carried the shotgun. They looked tired and wet, but still functional. Behind them Gerry was so tired he almost staggered. Even at a half mile I could tell he was exhausted. He was a plump, flabby, small-framed kid. All the muscle he had, he hired.

It had taken me about forty minutes to get to where I was from where they were. They were moving faster than I could, but Gerry slowed them down. I had at least a half hour, and I knew I had better make my stand here. I was nearly spent. I edged down the tree, holding my bad leg carefully away from me. When I reached the ground I had to ward Pearl off, to keep her from hurting my leg again.

"Unerring," I said. "You are unerring."

I moved slowly back down off the rise toward the stream. I made a wide circle as I went, being careful to avoid the path I'd taken up. The tracker would follow my path across the stream and up to the ridgeline before he discovered I'd doubled back. It should be enough time. If things worked out. I reached the stream and entered it about twenty yards below the place I'd crossed before. I waded upstream with Pearl on the bank, moving through the brush, glancing at me in puzzlement now and then, but enjoying the cascade of smells that she was encountering among the weeds along the bank. I took the ripening groundhog carcass from inside my jacket and tossed it across the stream to her. It landed five feet in front of her. She stopped. Dropped her head, raised her rear end, and put her front legs straight out in front of her. Then she pounced on it. Picked it up in her jaws, shook it a couple of times, and dashed off into the woods with it. Which is what I was hoping for.

At the point where I'd crossed before, standing in the water, I bent one branch and broke another, so that the tracker shouldn't miss it. Then I moved across to the far bank and pulled loose a small sapling, as if I had grabbed it to climb the bank and it had pulled loose. The water moved rapidly here, the streambed full up with the long rain. I went back to the far side of the stream, the one they'd come from, and edged myself in against the back, under the low sweep of a black spruce whose roots were half exposed in the stream bank.

I was hip deep in the water, half crouched against the bank. The cold water numbed my leg. The rain granulated the black surface of the stream. There were no rocks here, no snags, so that the fast water moved sleekly without any show of white. Pearl was out of sight, communing with her lunch. I took the Browning out and cocked it and waited.

In twenty minutes they arrived. The tracker first, moving easily through the cover. On his right hip I saw the nose of a holster poke down beneath the skirt of his mackinaw. He paused at the stream, looked both ways and across, saw the broken branch on the other side. His hair was long and black and wet, plastered by the rain against his skull. In profile he had a nose like Dick Tracy, and around the eye a hint of American Indian. I saw him nod to himself once, then step into the stream and walk across. Behind him came the other three: Maishe and Anthony, and the stranger with the sack. I had been right. It was a pillowcase, soaking wet now, and lumpy with canned goods in the bottom. Maishe looked back

165

once, hesitated, then shrugged and went into the stream. The other two went with him. They were all up the other side and thirty yards beyond before Gerry reached the stream. He was a mess. He was still wearing the camel's hair topcoat he'd worn in Beverly. It was belted up now, and the collar was up. But the coat was sodden with rain and probably added twenty pounds to his load. He was limping, and his breath was audible for ten yards, rasping in and out. Even in the cold rain his face was flushed, and he staggered occasionally as he struggled through the thick woods. He paused on the stream bank, gasping. Across the stream, Maishe turned and looked back. Gerry waved him on. Maishe shrugged again and started up toward the ridgeline after the other three. Gerry gasped in a big gulp of air and then edged into the stream. When he was halfway across I came out from under the tree and caught hold of him by the long modish hair at the back of his neck. I yanked him back toward me and jammed the Browning into his ear.

Gerry made a kind of yowling noise, and the people ahead stopped and turned. I held him motionless there in the stream with my gun screwed into his ear. The tracker hit the ground, rolled once. As he rolled I saw a flash of metallic movement. Then he was behind a rock outcropping with his handgun out. It was a big one, with a long barrel.

The other three stood motionless. The wiry guy with the pillowcase frozen in a sort of half crouch. The other two standing upright, looking at Gerry and me in the water. The noise of the stream and the sound of the rain was all there was.

"It ain't Richie," Maishe said finally.

166

"And proud of it," I said.

Gerry's voice was barely audible as it croaked out of his throat.

"Spenser?"

"Un huh."

Again silence. Pearl appeared on the rising ground opposite and sniffed at the pillowcase that the wiry guy was holding.

Nobody moved.

I said, "Which one of you wants to tell Joe that you were there when his kid got killed in the woods?"

"There's four of us, Spenser," Maishe said.

"How many did you start with?" I said.

No one spoke. Pearl continued to sniff carefully at the pillowcase, bending her neck and moving her feet a little to get a careful smell survey of the contents from every angle. The guy holding the pillowcase didn't look at her. His eyes were fixed on me.

"Where's Richie?" Maishe said.

Close to me I could hear Gerry's breath, wheezing through his throat as if there were very little room for it.

"Listen," I said. "Here's the deal. You four beat it. Gerry and I walk out of here alone, and when we get to the Mass Pike, I let him go."

"That's it?" Maishe said.

I nodded.

"And if we don't?"

"Then I drop Gerry like a stone and take my chances with you."

"How many rounds you got left?" Maishe said.

I didn't say anything.

Maishe looked at Anthony. Anthony had nothing to say.

167

"You drop Gerry and you got nothing left to bargain with," Maishe said.

I didn't say anything. Pearl had given up on the pillow-case and walked over to sniff at the tracker on the ground behind the granite. He reached back absently and scratched her ear with his free hand. Her tail wagged. Maishe shifted his feet a little. He looked at Gerry.

"What do you want, Gerry?" he said.

I spoke softly to Gerry, my mouth two inches from his left ear, the pressure of the Browning steady in his right one.

"I would like to kill you, Gerry. It would be a good thing for civilization. And it would be fun. I'll keep you alive if it gets me out of here. But you know that if the show starts, your brains will be floating in the water."

"How do I know you'll let me go?" His voice was little more than a hiss.

"Because I said I would."

Gerry was silent. Maishe spoke again.

"What do you want us to do, Gerry?"

"If I knew you'd let me go . . ." Gerry whispered.

I didn't say anything. Pearl left the tracker and moseyed happily down to the stream edge and drank noisily and long. Ripe woodchuck will give you a thirst.

Gerry raised his voice. "Do what he says."

"You want we should leave you?" Maishe said.

Gerry's voice was shrill with the effort of squeezing it out.

"Do what he says. I believe him. He'll let me go later."

What Gerry really believed was that I'd kill him now. We all knew that.

Maishe shrugged. The tracker got to his feet. He still

had the big revolver out but he let it slide down at his side. The guy with the pillowcase eased out of his crouch.

"Go back the way you came," I said. "Cross downstream. Keep going. If I see you or even hear you in the woods I will blow his brains out. And then you can explain to Joe how you let that happen, and who was in charge, and how four of you let one guy do it. Joe will be interested."

Nobody moved for a moment. Then Maishe said, "Fuck it," and the four of them began to drift back toward the stream, twenty yards or so down from where Gerry and I stood. I turned lowly as they went, keeping Gerry between us.

The tracker entered the streambed last. As he walked into the water he said to me, "Your dog?"

"Yeah."

"Nice dog."

"Thanks."

"Mass Pike's about three miles." He jerked his head. "Back that way. Stay on the ridgeline."

I nodded again. Then he was out of the stream.

"Maybe we'll see you down the road," he said.

I didn't answer and he was into the woods, and in a minute he was out of sight.

27

Gerry and I were strolling toward the Pike. My leg was hot and stiff and swollen tight against my jeans. I limped badly and my head swam periodically. I didn't mention this to Gerry. He walked three or four feet ahead of me. Struggling with his own limitations, barely aware of anything except the need to get air into his lungs and stay upright. Pearl hustled along in front of us, sometimes swinging far out of sight and then larupping back through the woods to prance in front of us with her tongue out, before she careened off again. She was able to go through the dense woods at nearly top speed. Groundhog must be nourishing.

I was having trouble concentrating. My mind kept moving back over things. I was cold and wet, but my body felt parched, and the pain in my leg pounded up and down my left side. Pearl came back to nuzzle my hand and went off again. I thought about beer. I had come down to New York, a lifetime ago, to fight a guy named Carmen Ramazottie, from Bayonne. We had fought a prelim at St. Nick's and I had put Carmen down with a very nice combination that my Uncle Bob had worked on with me. Bob and I stayed at a dump on the West Side called the Bristol, and the morning after the fight we checked out and took a subway to Brooklyn to see a ball game at Ebbets Field before we got the late bus home.

It was late August in New York. The subway was dense and sweaty and running slow. I had a headache and the right side of my face under the eye was puffy and darkening steadily from the reiterated application of Carmen's pretty good left jab. Coming up into the harsh city sun made my head hurt worse. I had been thirsty since the second round of last night's fight. I knew I was dehydrated and in time I'd catch up, but it didn't make me less thirsty. As we crossed Flatbush Avenue, the tar was soft from the sun, and the ballpark crowd was damp with sweat. Shirts clung. Bra straps chaffed. There were a lot of black faces in the crowd, come to see Jackie Robinson play.

Ebbets Field was small and idiosyncratic. It was a short 2976 feet to the right-field screen. The base of the scoreboard in right was angular, and Carl Furillo, and Dixie Walker before him, had made an art of playing to odd caroms off it. There were advertising signs on the outfield walls. The fans were close to the field, and after a game they could stream across the outfield and exit through the gate in deep center field.

The Cardinals were in, their gray road uniforms trimmed in red; Stan Musial and Red Schoendienst. We got seats behind first base while there was still batting practice to watch. I was old enough to drink in New York. In Boston I was still underage. We got two big paper cups of Schaefer beer and settled back.

The beer was cold from the tap and fresh. I felt it seep through me the way spring rain invigorates a flower.

171

In the top of the first inning Duke Snider did his little kick step and hit the ball into Bedford Avenue. My Uncle Bob and I toasted him with another beer. My headache was going. The throbbing in my cheek diminished. Stan Musial. Duke Snider. Cold beer in the sunshine. Only yesterday, when the world was young.

"I gotta rest," Gerry said.

My focus swam back onto him. He had slumped to the ground, his back against a birch tree, his legs sprawled before him, his arms limp at his side. I realized I'd lost track of him entirely. I didn't remember walking the last half mile. I didn't remember coming down the side of this gully.

I was lucky it was Gerry. The tracker would have brained me by now with a rock. I leaned against another birch trunk. If I sat down I wasn't sure I could get up.

"Get up," I said. Time was not my friend. I didn't have much of it left.

Gerry's head was sunk on his chest. He shook it silently.

"Okay," I said. "See you around."

My voice sounded like someone else's. Someone trying to sound perky. And failing. Pearl bounded over and jumped up to lap my face. She put one paw on my leg. I didn't scream. I held the tree with my left arm and fended her off with my right. I noticed that I was still holding the gun in my hand, but I'd let the hammer down. I didn't remember doing that. There was some nausea. It passed slowly, like a wave slowly easing back out to sea. When it was gone enough to move, I jerked my head at Pearl and started off.

Gerry said, "Hey."

I kept going.

He labored to his feet, using the tree trunk. He was

behind me now. I kept going. The gun in my right hand, hanging straight down, Pearl, ahead of me, nose to the forest floor, looking for groundhogs.

"Wait up," Gerry gasped.

It had become ludicrous. My hostage was chasing me. It was darkening and the drizzle had finally stopped when we reached the last rise and below us saw the traffic on the Pike. I took the leash from my pocket and whistled for Pearl. She dashed up and sat. She always dashed up and sat when she saw the leash. To her it meant a walk. Even when she was on a walk. I hooked the leash onto her collar. And we started down the slope. Pearl strained against the leash and my leg hurt exceptionally as I went downhill on it, bracing against Pearl's tug. To my right Gerry started to run toward the highway and fell and rolled noisily through the brush for maybe thirty feet before he stopped and struggled up and kept moving.

Most of the cars had their headlights on, though it wasn't really dark yet. And they paraded by swiftly and sporadically, a pageant of ordinariness, the people in them rushing to dinner, or a late meeting, unwounded, unfeverish, unarmed, dry, and at worst maybe a little stiff from their long commute.

The chances of flagging a ride were negligible, but sooner or later a state cop would cruise by, and he'd stop. If he saw us. I looped Pearl's leash over my wrist so that if I passed out she wouldn't wander off into the traffic. Gerry was standing limply ten feet down the highway. He wasn't looking at me. His head was down. His eyes may have been closed; I couldn't see.

"Walk away from me," I said. "That way. Keep going until you're out of sight. If I see you again I'll kill you."

Gerry had no words. He simply turned in the direction

I'd pointed and began to stumble along the highway, his head down, weaving as he walked, as if he were drunk. Pearl was close to my leg, shying closer every time a car passed, stirring the leaves and dust along the margin of the roadbed.

I couldn't remember now who had won that baseball game. Cardinals or Dodgers? It had probably mattered greatly then; it mattered now not at all. I felt myself begin to dissolve. I frowned. I concentrated on looking up the Pike at the oncoming headlights. It would be harder to spot me if I keeled over. It would be harder to spot me as it got darker. I looked down the road after Gerry Broz. I couldn't see him. The turnpike curved fifty yards ahead and he was around the curve now. I holstered the Browning. Gerry wouldn't have the energy to circle back and jump me. Nor, probably, now that he was alone, the balls. I remembered that once; I had seen Jackie Robinson steal home. Pigeon-toed, elbows pumping, under the tag. He was dead now. Been dead a long time. Died a young man. *He lit up the sky,* my Uncle Bob used to say. The headlights blurred in the mist. Except there wasn't any mist. The rain had stopped an hour ago. The first time Robinson had taken the field, Red Barber had said in his soft Southern voice on the radio, *He is very definitely brunette.* One pair of the blurred headlights swept over me. A car swung up onto the shoulder. The door opened and Hawk got out.

"You are very definitely brunette," I said.

Then Hawk blurred too.

I heard myself say, "Take the dog."

And then I didn't hear anything. Or see anything, except darkness visible.

174

28

Someone said, "Where's the dog?"

Somebody else said, "In the car with a soup bone."

"On the leather seats?" someone said.

"You bled all over them already," someone else said. "Figured it didn't matter anymore."

My eyes opened. Hawk was standing at the foot of the bed, wearing a black leather jacket over a black turtleneck. He leaned forward and rested his forearms on the bed rail and I could see the butt of his gun under his arm where the jacket fell open.

"How come you were out riding around on the Pike in western Mass?" I said. It had been me speaking all along, but I just realized it.

"Paul told me what happened," Hawk said. "I looked at a map, figured you'd get in the woods and loop for the highway. What I woulda done."

"So you been cruising it," I said.

"Un huh. Lee exit to the New York line and back, two tanks of gas."

"Paul's okay?"

"He at your place. So's his momma and her honey."

175

"My place?"

"You not using it," Hawk said. "Had to stash them someplace."

I shifted in the bed. There was an IV in the back of
my left hand, held in place by tape. The tube ran to a
drip bottle on a stand. My leg felt sore, but it wasn't
throbbing anymore, and it didn't feel distended. I
looked around the room. It was private. There was a silent television on a high shelf opposite, and the usual
hospital apparatus on the walls, blood pressure gauges,
and oxygen outlets, and spigots for purposes unclear to
the lay public.

"I'm in a hospital," I said.

"Wow," Hawk said.

"I'm a trained observer," I said. "Where?"

"Pittsfield," Hawk said.

"Susan?"

"I called her," Hawk said. "She on the way, bringing
you some clothes."

I was wearing a hospital johnny. I glanced at the night
table.

"Wallet's in the nightstand," Hawk said. "Got your
gun."

"How am I?"

"You not going to die, you not going to lose the leg, your
personality not going to improve."

"So, two out of three," I said.

"Some people say none out of three," Hawk said.
"Where's Gerry?"

"Left him on the turnpike," I said. "Walking toward
Stockbridge."

"Want to tell me about it?" Hawk said.

I did.

"Been about thirty hours," Hawk said. "Figure Gerry be home by now."

I raised the sheet and looked at my leg. It was bandaged thickly, around the thigh. The part that showed looked a little bruised but not too puffy.

"Cops been around?" I said.

"Yeah. Hospital called them when they saw the gunshot wound. I told them you was out in the woods with the dog while I waiting in Stockbridge. When you didn't come back I went and found you."

"They believe you?"

"No."

"Don't blame them," I said.

A thin-faced, dark-haired nurse came in.

"Awake," she said.

"Yes."

She smiled without thinking about it and took out an electronic thermometer and took my temperature. She read it and nodded to herself and wrote something on her clipboard. She took my pulse, and my blood pressure, and noted those.

"We hungry yet?" she said.

"I am," I said. "How about you?"

Another automatic smile. "I'll have them bring you something."

She located a remote control unit attached to a cord on the bedside table.

"Want to sit up?"

"Sure."

I noticed that during her time in the room she had not looked at Hawk. But she was aware of him. I could see the awareness in her shoulders and the way she held her neck. She showed me the remote.

"We push this to sit up," she said. "And this turns on our television. And if we need a nurse we push this one."

I said, "Are you going to get into bed with me? Or is this *we* stuff just a tease?"

She looked blankly at me for a moment. Then she grinned.

"Let's wait until your leg is better," she said.

"That's what they all say."

"Oh, I doubt that," she said. "My name is Felicia. You want me"—she grinned—"for medical reasons, press the button."

She watched me while I raised the bed into a nearly sitting position. Then she turned to go. At the door she glanced back at Hawk. He smiled at her and she flushed and went out of the room. In maybe a minute she was back and with her came a young guy wearing a brown Sears and Roebuck suit. He was nearly bald, and what little was left he wore cut very short.

"Officer deShayes wants to see you," she said, and whisked her white skirt back out the door without looking again at Hawk.

DeShayes showed me a badge that said Pittsfield Police on it. Then he put the badge away and took out a small spiral notebook with a red cover.

"Feeling okay?" he said.

"On top of the world," I said.

"Good," he said. "Good. Just some routine questions here. We always have to follow up on gunshot wounds, you know."

"Yeah."

He glanced once at Hawk, who had retired to an uncomfortable chair under the television set and appeared
to go to sleep. Now that I was sitting up, I could see that
his jeans were black and he wore them tucked inside
black cowboy boots.

"Friend of yours?" deShayes said.

"Darth Vader," I said.

DeShayes nodded. "So how did you come by this gunshot wound?"

"Self-inflicted," I said. "Accidental."

"Un huh. Could you describe the events which caused
you to perpetrate this self-inflicted wound?"

"Sure. I was walking the dog, in the woods, and thought
I'd take a little target practice. And accidentally shot myself."

"And where is this dog now?"

"In his car," I said, nodding at Hawk.

"And the gun with which the wound was inflicted?"

"He's got it," I said. Without opening his eyes Hawk
produced my gun from inside his jacket and held it out
toward deShayes. DeShayes took it and sniffed the barrel
and popped out the magazine and cleared the round from
the chamber. It flipped onto the bed near my hip. He
thumbed the shells out of the magazine, onto the bed
beside the first one. He nodded to himself, the way the
nurse had after she'd taken my temperature.

"You're from Boston?" deShayes said. He put the
empty magazine back in my gun, put the gun on the night
table, picked up the five shells, and dropped them into his
suitcoat pocket.

"Yes."

"A private detective."

179

"Yes."

"Licensed to carry this gun?"

"Yes."

"Do you happen to have the license with you?"

"In the wallet, in the drawer," I said.

He reached into the drawer and took out my wallet and handed it to me.

"Take out the gun permit please, and your ID."

I did, and handed them to him. He looked them over carefully and made a couple of notes in his little spiral notebook with his blue Bic pen. Then he handed the stuff back to me.

"Live in Boston?" he said.

"Yes."

"Where you staying out here?"

"Just came out for the day," I said.

"Why?"

"Take the dog in the woods. She loves the woods."

"Two-hour drive to walk the dog?"

"She's a good dog," I said.

He nodded. His face was blank.

"That's a Browning isn't it?" DeShayes nodded at the black automatic lying on the night table.

"Yes."

"Don't they usually hold thirteen rounds in the clip?"

"Yeah."

"There's only four rounds in your clip and one in the chamber."

"I fired off eight rounds target shooting."

"One of which hit you, according to the surgeon, in the back middle quadrant of your left thigh."

"Embarrassing, isn't it."

180

"Actually I think it's more than embarrassing, sir. I think it's bullshit," deShayes said.

I didn't say anything. Hawk remained peaceful with his eyes closed. His legs straight out in front of him, crossed at the ankles.

"How'd you get out here?" deShayes said.

"Drove out, separate cars."

"And where is your car now?"

"Where I parked it, I hope. In the parking lot at the Red Lion."

DeShayes made some more notes.

"Stockbridge police found a car registered to you, this morning, parked in front of a house in town. Tires had been shot out, and most of the windows in the house had been shot out. They're still digging bullets out of the plaster."

"Son of a gun," I said. "Somebody must have hot-wired it."

"No sign of that," deShayes said.

"Car thieves are getting very clever these days, aren't they?"

DeShayes didn't comment. He wrote another thing in his little notebook.

"You have anything to add?" he said.

"You know what I know," I said.

"Sure," deShayes said. "They tell me you'll be here awhile. If you decide to leave before I get back to you, give me a call." He handed me a card that read Detective Joseph E. deShayes.

"What's the *E* for?" I said.

"Make sure you check with me before you leave," deShayes said. "Got it?"

181

"I think so," I said. "He can help me with the hard parts." I nodded at Hawk.

DeShayes stood. He took my five cartridges out of his pocket and put them in an ashtray on the night table.

"Be careful with these," he said.

29

I dined on chicken broth and raspberry Jell-O, which was an improvement on acorns and chokecherries, but only a small one. After I ate I fell asleep and when I woke up Susan was there. She had on black jeans that fitted the form of her leg, and low-heeled boots that came above midcalf, and a white silk blouse which she wore with the top two buttons open. Her black hair was thick and shiny, and her eyes looked extra large and shadowed in the odd hospital lighting.

Hawk was still in his chair. Susan had pulled a straight chair near the bed and sat in it. She was reading a copy of *Metropolitan Home*. Squinting a little, turning the magazine as she read, trying to catch the light. I lay quietly for a little while watching her.

"Hey," I said.

She raised her head from the magazine and smiled at me, and leaned forward and kissed me on the mouth.

"Hey," she said.

I fumbled for the remote and found it and pushed the button and raised myself up in the bed.

"How are you?" Susan said.

"Fit as a fiddle and ready for love. I could jump over the moon up above."

Susan smiled. "How nice," she said, "that your ordeal has not aged you."

I put my hand out and she took it and we were quiet, holding hands.

Felicia came back in. "Well," she said, "I see we're awake again."

"Felicia identifies with me," I said to Susan.

"Dr. Good will be in to see you in a little while."

"Is his first name Feel?" I said.

"No," Felicia said, "I think it's Jeffrey. He's the chief resident."

Felicia took my temperature and my blood pressure and pulse. She had me lean forward while she smoothed the sheets and plumped the pillows. While this was going on a guy in a white coat came in with a stethoscope hanging loosely from his neck.

"Hi," he said. "I'm Jeff Good. I was in the ER when you came in."

I introduced Susan and started to introduce Hawk.

"I met this gentleman when he brought you in," Dr. Good said. "A very strong guy, it would appear. He carried you in like you were a child."

"He's childlike in many ways," Susan said.

Dr. Good smiled without really paying much attention and pulled back the sheet to look at my leg. He touched it lightly here and there, nodding to himself. The place was full of people who nodded to themselves. Everybody knew stuff. Nobody was saying.

"What's the diagnosis?" I said.

184

"Blood loss and infection, both the result of a single gunshot wound in your left thigh. Exhaustion. We're pumping you full of antibiotics now, and I think we've got the infection under control. We gave you some blood already."

"When can I go home?"

Good shrugged. "Another day, probably, if your fever stays down, and you promise to see someone in Boston, and stay off the thing for a while."

"Sure," I said.

"Got everything you need?"

"I could use something to eat besides chicken broth and Jell-O."

"Is that what they're feeding you?" Good shook his head. He looked at Felicia, who stood worshipfully aside, gazing at him. "Can we get him a real meal?"

"Of course, Doctor. No restrictions?"

"No."

He nodded at me and went out. Felicia hurried after him.

"I'd say your chances with Felicia aren't as good as they looked," I said to Hawk.

Hawk shrugged. "It's 'cause I'm not trying," he said.

"Would you care to tell me how you came to be here in the hospital?" Susan said. "I've had some high points from Hawk, but I'd like the full treatment if you're not too tired."

"Certainly," I said. "It's a compelling story, which I tell elegantly."

Hawk stood up from his chair. He seemed to do this without effort. In fact without movement. One moment he was sitting and then he was standing.

185

"I've already heard the story," Hawk said. "I think I'll go walk Pearl. Gun's in the drawer. Round in the chamber."

I opened the night-table drawer as he left and saw my gun. Hawk had reloaded it. I left the drawer open.

Susan looked at the gun and at me and didn't say anything.

"We found Patty," I said. "And Rich. And Gerry Broz found us."

"How?"

"Patty told somebody," I said.

"God, she must feel awful."

"Maybe," I said. "I think she's so needy, and so desperate, that she can't feel anything but the need."

Susan nodded. "So what happened?"

I told her. She listened quietly. I always loved it when I had a story to tell her, because her attention was complete and felt like sunlight. Hawk came back just before the end.

"Pearl actually killed and ate a groundhog?" Susan said.

"Showed that soup bone no mercy, either," Hawk said.

"Let's not spread this around Cambridge," I said. "The Vegetarian Sisterhood will picket her."

"And you let Gerry Broz go?" Susan said.

"Had to. I didn't know how long I was going to stay on my feet. If I passed out while he was there, he'd have shot me with my own gun."

"Could have shot him," Hawk said.

I shrugged.

"Could you do that?" Susan said. "Just shoot him like that?"

I shrugged again.

"Gerry could," Hawk said. "Spenser keels over, Gerry shoots him while he's laying there."

"Will he . . ." Susan stopped. "I don't know how to say it. Will he be less dangerous to you because you let him go?"

"Pretty to think so," Hawk said.

Susan looked at me. I shook my head.

"Hawk's right," I said. "Gerry will have to come for me. He can't stand to have been—the way he would think of it—humiliated in front of his people."

"Maybe then you should have shot him," Susan said.

"As a practical matter," I said.

"Yes," Susan said.

"I love you when you're bloodthirsty," I said.

"Don't patronize me," Susan said. "You know I'm not bloodthirsty, but I love you. I can be very practical about you if I must be, very bloodthirsty if you prefer."

"I know," I said. "I take back bloodthirsty. But . . ." I spread my hands. "Before all this happened I talked to Joe."

"Joe Broz?"

"Yeah. Gerry's father. He's worried about the kid. It's his only kid and he's no good and Joe knows it."

"He ought to know it," Susan said. "What chance did his son have being the child of a mobster?"

"Joe doesn't mind that he's a mobster too," I said. "Joe likes that. What kills Joe is that he's such a crapola mobster."

"He feel sorry for Joe," Hawk said.

We were all silent.

Finally Susan said, "Would you have killed him, Hawk?"

"Absolutely," Hawk said.

"He's dangerous still?"

"He gonna come for us," Hawk said.

At which point the ineffable Felicia came in with my supper.

30

"Whatever happened to that Harvard woman you used to date?" Susan said.

"Daisy or Cindy?" Hawk said. "They both from Harvard."

"Well, tell me about both of them," Susan said. "I didn't realize you had this passion for intellectuals."

"I'se here with you, missy."

"True," Susan said. "Which one was Daisy?"

I probed the sliced turkey with my fork. It was densely blanketed with a dark gravy.

"Daisy is the redhead, taught black studies." Hawk's face was without expression. Susan raised her eyebrows.

"Yeah," Hawk said. "This a while ago. Everybody teaching black studies. Red-haired broad with freckles, grew up in Great Neck, Long Island. Only black people she ever saw were from the Long Island Expressway driving through Jamaica."

"I assume her emphasis tended toward the more theoretical aspects of the black experience," Susan said.

I ate some turkey. It was pretty tender, but the gravy was hard to chew.

"She'd read *Invisible Man* six times," Hawk said. "Everything Angela Davis ever wrote. Told me she ashamed of being white. Told me she thought maybe she black in another life."

I tried some mashed potatoes. They were chewy, too.

"An African princess perhaps?" I said. It came out muffled because I was still gnawing on the mashed potatoes.

"Amazing you should guess that," Hawk said.

"Funny, isn't it," I said—and paused and tried to swallow the potato, and succeeded on the second try—"how people almost never seem to have been four-dollar whores in a Cape Town crib in another life."

"Anyway, me and Daisy used to go to The Harvest for dinner," Hawk said.

"The Harvest?" Susan said.

"Un huh," Hawk said.

I put a forkful of lukewarm succotash in my mouth, chewed it aggressively and swallowed it, hoping to tamp down the potatoes a bit.

"My God," Susan said. "The thought of you at The Harvest."

"Un huh," Hawk said.

"People in The Harvest talk about Proust," Susan said. "And Kierkegaard."

"Daisy talk about my elemental earthiness," Hawk said.

"And they talk about whether they have a date for Saturday night," Susan said. "And sometimes they discuss your sign."

"You been going there without me?" I said.

"Certainly. While you're out waltzing through the woods with your faithful dog, I'm at the bar in The Harvest, wearing a beret, reading *Paris-Match,* sipping white wine, and smoking imported cigarettes with my hand turned the wrong way."

"Waiting for Mister Right?" I said.

"Yes. In a seersucker jacket."

"Mister Right don't wear no seersucker jacket," Hawk said.

"Sandals?" Susan said.

Hawk shook his head.

"Chinos and Bass Weejuns?"

"Nope."

"Does he wear his sweater draped over his shoulder like a shawl?"

"Positively not," Hawk said.

"He wears blue blazers with brass buttons," I said. "And has a nose that's encountered adversity."

"And an eighteen-inch neck?" Susan said.

"That's the guy," I said.

"Yes, it is," Susan said.

"Other woman was Cindy Astor," Hawk said. "Taught at the Kennedy School. Only female full professor they had when I was with her. Specialized in Low Country politics. Had a law degree, a master's in English, a Ph.D. in Dutch history. Used to work for the State Department, spent some time at the American Embassy in Brussels. Smart."

I worked on the turkey with gravy some more. In a little paper cup next to it was some pink applesauce—maybe.

"Smarter than you?" Susan said.

"No."

"And did you and she dine at The Harvest?"

Hawk shook his head.

"Her place mostly. Sometimes we'd go to the Harvard Faculty Club, get some boiled food."

"Were you impressed with the Harvard Faculty Club?" Susan said.

I knew she knew that Hawk was never impressed with anything, and I knew how much she was enjoying the image of Hawk eating haddock and boiled potatoes among the icons of Harvard intellection.

"Man asked me once what I did for a living," Hawk said. His voice sank into a perfect mimic of the upper-class Yankee honk.

" 'What exactly is it you do, sir?' man say to me. I say, 'I'm in security and enforcement, my good man.' And the man say to me 'How fascinating.' And I say, 'More fascinating if you the enforcer than if you the enforcee.' And he look at me sort of strange and say, 'Yes, yes, certainly,' and he hustle off to the bar, order a double Manhattan. Two cherries."

I ate the dessert. It might have been vanilla pudding.

"But you weren't in love with these women?"

"No."

"Think you'll ever fall in love?"

"Probably not," Hawk said.

"You might," Susan said.

"Maybe I can't," Hawk said.

My eyes were heavy and I leaned back against the pillow.

I heard Susan say, "I hadn't thought of that."

And then I was asleep.

31

Pearl was hurrying around my apartment, sniffing everything, including Rich Beaumont and Patty Giacomin, which neither of them liked much.

"Can you get Pearl to settle down?" Paul said.

"I could speak to her, but she'd continue to do what she wants, and I'd look ineffectual. My approach is to endorse everything she does."

Susan said, "Come here, Pearl." And Pearl went over to her, and Susan gave her a kiss on the mouth, and Pearl wagged her tail, and lapped Susan's face, and turned and went back and sniffed at Patty.

"Isn't that cute," I said.

"Never mind about the damn dog," Beaumont said. "We got a problem here and we need to solve it."

He had helped himself to one of my shirts, which was too big for him, and he hadn't shaved. He looked a little seedier than he had in Stockbridge. He glanced once, uneasily, toward Hawk, leaning on the wall near the front hall entry. Hawk smiled at him cheerily.

"I mean, we can't stay here forever," Beaumont said.

"I thought of that too," I said. "What's your plan?"

"I don't know," Beaumont said. "Can you help us out?"

"He already did that," Paul said.

"Yeah," Beaumont said. "Yeah, sure. I know. I mean, shit, you got yourself shot helping us out. It's not like I don't know that and appreciate it."

"We both do," Patty said. She was sitting beside Beaumont on the couch, holding his hand. "We both appreciate it so much."

"I was you I'd go to the cops," I said.

"Cops?"

"Yeah. You must have enough to trade them for protection."

"Christ—the stuff I got is *on* the cops. Who we paid, when, how much. I wouldn't last a day."

"I'll put you in touch with cops you can trust," I said.

"And they'll have me guarded by cops they can trust, and so on. Sure. But what if they're wrong, or what if you're wrong?"

"I'm not wrong."

"It's a big world," Beaumont said. "We got money to go anywhere in it. All you got to do is get us out of this city."

"How about you, Mom?" Paul said.

Patty shook her head and clutched onto Beaumont's hand.

"You want to go anywhere in the world with him?"

Patty glanced around the room; nobody said anything. She pressed her face against Beaumont's shoulder.

"Sure she does," Beaumont said. "She loves me."

"A crook, Mom? A guy that carries a gun and steals money and is a fugitive from the damned mob?"

Patty sat up straight and rested her clenched fists on her thighs. "It's not so easy for a girl to be alone, Paulie."

194

Paul said, "You don't go off with a goddamned gangster because it's hard to be alone. If you can't be alone, you can't be anybody. Haven't you ever found that out? To be with somebody first you got to be with you."

"Oh, Paulie, all that psychobabble. I never thought you should have gone to that shrink in the first place."

"And where do you get off calling me a gangster, kid?" Beaumont asked.

"You don't like 'gangster'? How about 'thief'? That better?"

"I don't have to take that shit," Beaumont said.

"Please," Patty said. "Please. Paulie, I can't make it alone. When your father left me I thought I'd die. I have to be with somebody. Rich loves me. There's nothing wrong with being loved. Rich would stand on his head for me."

"Jesus Christ, Ma," Paul said. "My father leaving you was the best chance you had. You didn't love him. He was a creep. You had a chance and instead you went to another creep, and then another. Get away from this guy, be alone for a while. I'll help you. Find out who you are. You could have a decent guy someday if you got your goddamned head together."

"Who you calling a creep?" Beaumont said. He leaned forward as if he were going to stand. Leaning on the wall, Hawk cleared his throat. Beaumont looked at him and froze, then sank back on the couch.

Patty pounded both fists on her thighs. "Goddamn you! I found a man who loves me. I won't let him go. Not for you and all your highfaluting shrink ideas. You don't know what it's like to be abandoned."

Paul was silent for a moment. No one else spoke. Pearl

195

got up from where she had been sitting near Susan and walked over to sniff at Hawk's pants leg.

"Well, not like I mean," Patty said. "I mean, sure, you had a tough time when you were a kid maybe, but we took care of you. You went to good schools. Now, you turned out fine, see that. How bad a mother could I be? Look at you. Got a career, got a girlfriend. I must have done something right."

Pearl seemed to have found out whatever she wanted to find out by sniffing Hawk's pants leg. She turned and came back across the room and sat down next to me and leaned against my leg. Unerringly she leaned against the bad one. I flinched a little and shifted.

"What I got, Ma," Paul said, "is me. And I didn't get that from you. I got that from him." He nodded toward me.

"Oh, God, it makes me tired to listen to you. It's all words. I don't know what they all mean. I know that Rich loves me. If he goes, I'm going with him. You don't know, none of you do, what it's like being a woman."

"Some of us do," Susan said.

"Yes—and you've got a man," Patty said.

"We have each other," Susan said.

"Well, I've got Rich."

"Happy as a fish with a new bicycle," I said softly.

Paul was silent. He stared at his mother; nobody said anything. Beaumont stirred a little on the couch.

"It's kind of no-class, kid," he said, "to wash the family linen in front of strangers like this, you know?"

Paul paid no attention to him. He was still looking at his mother. She had linked her arm through Beaumont's and was pressing her cheek, defiantly, this time, against his shoulder. She looked back at him unflinchingly. They held the stare, and as they held it Paul began to nod slowly.

"Okay," he said. "That was my last shot. I've been talking to you for two days. You do what you need to do. You are my mother, and I love you. If you need something from me, you know where I am."

Patty got up. "Oh, Paulie," she said and put her arms around him and pressed her face into his chest. She cried quietly, and he held her tight and patted her back, but his gaze over her shoulder was deeply silent and focused on something far down a dwindling perspective.

I looked at Beaumont. "No cops?" I said.

"No cops."

"Does it bother you at all that if you take off I'm going to have to deal with Broz?"

"You could take off, too," Beaumont said. "You need some money, I can pay you for what you did."

I shook my head.

"Then I can't help you," Beaumont said. "I got to take care of my own ass."

"And hers," I said.

"Of course," Beaumont said.

"I'd have to deal with Gerry anyway," I said. I looked at Hawk.

"Where you want to go?" he said to Beaumont.

Beaumont hesitated and looked at me, and then at Hawk. He decided.

"Montreal," he said.

Hawk nodded. "Get your things," he said.

32

I was in my office on Monday morning, with my office calendar, figuring out how many days were left until baseball season began. The door opened and Vinnie Morris came in and stood aside, and Joe Broz came in, followed by Gerry Broz. I opened the second drawer in my desk, near my right hand where I kept a spare gun.

"Broz and Broz," I said. "Double the fun."

Vinnie started to close the door and Joe shook his head.

"Wait in the car, Vinnie," he said.

"Joe?" Vinnie said.

"In the car, Vinnie. This is family."

"I'm not family, Joe?"

Broz shook his head again.

"No," he said. "Not quite, Vinnie. Not on this."

"I'll be in the corridor," Vinnie said.

Again Broz shook his head.

"No, Vinnie—*in the car.*"

Vinnie hesitated with the door half open, his hand on the knob. He was looking at Joe.

"Go, Vinnie. Do it."

Vinnie nodded and went out without looking at me and shut the door behind him. Gerry started to pull up one of my client chairs.

"No," Broz said. "Don't sit. We ain't here to sit."

"Jesus, you got to tell me everything to do. Stand? Sit? In front of this creep?"

"Spenser ain't no creep," Joe said. "One of your many problems, Gerry. You don't think about who you're dealing with."

"So whaddya going to do, explain him to me?"

Joe stared at me. It was almost as if we were friends, which we weren't. Then he inhaled slowly and turned to look at his son.

"Man gave you a break," Joe said. "He could have dropped you in the woods."

"He knew what would happen to him if he did," Gerry said.

Gerry was a little taller than his father, but softer. He was dressed on the cutting edge with baggy, stone-washed jeans and an oversized black leather jacket with big lapels. Joe wore a dark suit and a gray tweed overcoat with a black velvet collar. Both were hatless.

"What would have happened?" Joe said.

"You'd have had Vinnie pop him."

Joe nodded without saying anything. I waited. At the moment this had to do with Joe and Gerry.

"And what should I do now?" Joe said.

"Since when do you ask me, Pa? You don't ask me shit. You asking me now?"

Joe nodded.

"Okay—we'll have Vinnie pop him, like you shoulda done a long time ago."

Joe was looking only at Gerry. Gerry's eyes shifted back and forth between Joe, and, obliquely, me.

"You think he's got to go, Gerry?"

199

Gerry shifted, glanced again at me, and away again.

"For crissake, Pa, I already told you. Yeah. He's trouble. He's in the way. We'd have had Beaumont out west if he hadn't been there."

"And you chased him into the woods with four guys besides yourself, and he took you."

"Pa."

"With a fucking bullet in him."

"Pa, for crissake. You gotta do this here, in front of him?"

Gerry's face was flushed. And his voice sounded thick.

"And he got away with it," Joe said. His voice was flat, scraped bare of feeling by the effort of saying it.

"Pa." Gerry's breathing was very short. Each exhalation was audible, as if the air was too thin. "Pa, don't."

Joe nodded vigorously.

"I got to, Gerry," he said. "I thought about this for three four days now. I haven't thought about anything else. I got to."

The flush left Gerry's face. It became suddenly very pale, and his voice pitched up a notch.

"What? You got to what?"

"One of these days I'm going to die and the thing will be yours. The whole fucking thing."

Gerry was frozen, staring at his father. I could have been in Eugene, Oregon, for all I mattered right then.

"And when you get it you got to be able to take care of it or they'll bite you in two, you unnerstand, like a fucking chum fish, they'll swallow you."

Gerry seemed to lean backwards. He opened his mouth and closed it and opened it again and said, "Vinnie . . ."

"I wish you was like Vinnie," Joe said. "But you don't

200

take care of this thing by having a guy do it for you. Vinnie can't be tough for you."

"You think I need Vinnie? You think Vinnie has to take care of me? Fuck Vinnie. I'm sick of Vinnie. Who's your son anyway, for crissake? Fucking Vinnie? Is he your son? Whyn't you leave the fucking thing to him, he's so great?"

"Because he's not my son," Joe said.

All of us were still. Outside, there was sound of traffic on Berkeley Street, dimmed by distance and walls. Inside my office the silence swelled.

Finally Gerry spoke. His voice was small and flat. "What do you want me to do?"

"I want you to deal with him," Joe said and tilted his head toward me.

"I been telling you that," Gerry said. "I been saying that Vinnie—"

"No," Joe said. "Not Vinnie. You. You got to deal with Spenser. You run our thing and there will be people worse to deal with than him. You got to be able to do it, not have it done. You think I started out with Vinnie?"

"You had Phil," Gerry said.

"Before Phil, before anybody, there was me. Me. And after me there's got to be you. Not Vinnie, not four guys from Providence. You."

"You want me to take him out," Gerry said. "You're telling me that right in front of him."

"Right in front," Joe said. "So he knows. So there's no back-shooting and sneaking around. You tell him he's gone and then you take him out."

"Right now?" Gerry's voice was barely audible.

"Now you tell him. You take him out when you're ready to."

"Joe," I said.

They both turned and stared at me as if I'd been eavesdropping.

"He can't," I said. "He's not good enough. You'll get him killed."

Joe was looking sort of up at me with his chin lowered. He shook his head as if there was something buzzing in his ears.

"They'll take everything away from him," Joe said.

"He could find other work," I said.

Joe shook his head.

"I don't want to kill him, Joe," I said.

"You motherfucker," Gerry said. His voice cracked a little as it went up. "You won't kill me. I'll fucking kill you, you fuck."

"Talks good, too," I said to Joe.

"You heard him," Joe said. "Be looking for him. Not Vinnie, not me, Gerry. You heard him."

"Goddamn it, Joe," I said. "Let him up. He's not good enough."

"You heard him," Joe said and turned on his heel and went out of the room. Gerry and I looked at each other for a silent pause, then Gerry turned on his heel, just like his poppa, and went out. Nobody shut the door.

I sat for a while and looked at the open door and the empty corridor. I looked at the S & W .357 in the open drawer by my right hand. I closed the drawer, got up, and closed the door. Then I went back and sat down and swiveled my chair and looked out the window for a while.

Spenser, rite of passage.

33

Paul and I were drinking beer at the counter in my kitchen. It was late. Pearl was strolling about the apartment with a yellow tennis ball clamped in her jaws. She was working it the way a pitcher chews tobacco.

"So that's her," Paul said. "That's my mom."

"Yes, it is," I said.

"Not exactly June Cleaver."

"Nobody is," I said.

"Not exactly an adult woman," Paul said.

"No," I said.

"Do you know where Hawk took them?"

"No."

"I wonder if I'll ever hear from her."

"Yes," I said. "I think you will."

"Because she'll miss her baby boy?"

I shrugged.

"Because the relationship with Beaumont won't last and she'll need help and she'll call me."

"Yes."

"You think Beaumont loves her?"

"I think he has some kind of feeling for her," I said. "But love is not usually an issue for guys like Beaumont."

"She's crazy about him."

"Maybe."

"Or she needs him, or someone like him."

Pearl came by and nudged my arm. I tried to ignore her. I didn't want to play ball right now. She nudged again and made a low sound.

"Always a loser," Paul said. "From my father on. Always some flashy second-rate jerk. Like she's not good enough for a decent guy and she knows it, or chooses these guys to punish herself for being . . . whatever she is: sexual, irresponsible, a bad wife, a bad mother, a bad girl instead of the boy her father wanted? How the fuck do I know? Sometimes I think I've talked too long with the shrinks."

"Saved your life at one point," I said.

"Sure," Paul said. He drank some beer from the bottle. His elbows were on the counter and he had to dip his neck to get enough tilt to the bottle. Pearl made another low sound and nudged my arm again. I patted her head and she shied away, hoping to lure me into a grab for the ball. I was too smart for her. I drank a little beer instead.

"Well, we found her," Paul said.

"Yes."

"I needed to find her."

"I know."

"I won't have to find her again."

Pearl stood close to my knee and dropped the tennis ball suggestively and looked at me with her head canted to the right. The ball bounced twice and lay still on the floor. I paid no heed.

"She has no control," Paul said. He bounced his clenched fist gently on the counter top. "She has never taken control of her life—*Who are you? I'm the woman in that man's life*—Jesus Christ!"

"She needs to be alone for a while," I said.

"Of course she does," Paul said. "You think she ever will be?"

"Not by choice," I said.

"She doesn't do anything by choice," Paul said.

"You're not like her," I said.

"Christ what a gene pool, though, her and old Mel, the paterfamilias."

"You're not like your father either," I said.

We were quiet. Pearl had picked up the ball again and was mouthing it at me. Paul got off the stool and got two more beers out of the refrigerator and opened them and handed me one.

"Why don't you and Susan get married?" Paul said.

"I'm not sure," I said. "It's probably in the area of *if it's not broke, don't fix it.*"

"You love her."

"Absolutely."

"You're so sure," Paul said.

"Like I know I'm alive," I said.

"I'm not sure everyone is like you," Paul said.

"Probably just as well," I said. "But . . ." I shrugged.

"I don't know. I don't know if I really love Paige."

I nodded.

"You don't know either, do you?" Paul said.

"If you really love Paige? No, I don't."

"No advice?"

"None."

"It helped, you know, finding my mother," Paul said.

"I know."

"Metaphorically, as well as really," he said.

"I know."

Pearl had the ball again and nudged my arm and mur-

205

mured at me. I made a lightning move for the ball, and she moved her head half an inch and I missed. She growled and wagged her tail. I grabbed again. She moved her head again. If I'd had her reflexes I'd have beaten Joe Walcott . . . and my nose would be straight. On the third try I grabbed her collar and held her while I pried the ball loose. Then I fired it into the living room where it ricocheted around with Pearl in lickety-split pursuit, her claws scrabbling on the hardwood floors. She got it and brought it back and nudged my arm and made a low sound.

"You needed to find your mother, and you did and you got the chance to look straight at her and now you know what she's like," I said. "That's progress."

"The truth will set you free," Paul said. His voice was angry.

"Not necessarily," I said. "But *pretend* sure as hell doesn't do it."

Paul turned and looked at me for a minute and then raised his bottle and drank and put it back down on the counter top and grinned.

"Malt does more than Milton can," he said, "to justify God's ways to man."

Pearl nudged my arm again. I grabbed at the ball. And missed.

CHAPTER

34

I was drinking coffee and eating donuts and reading the *Globe* while I sat in my car in the parking lot of the Dunkin' Donuts shop on Market Street in Allston. Pearl was in the backseat, with her head on my right shoulder, and every once in a while I would give her a piece of donut. I had bought with that in mind, so there were enough. I was studying *Calvin & Hobbes* when Vinnie Morris opened the door on the passenger side and got in.

"I been looking for you," he said.

"You been following me," I said.

Vinnie shrugged.

"Usually they don't make me," he said.

"Usually they're not me," I said. "You alone?"

"Yeah."

I didn't double-check him in the rearview mirror. Vinnie would kill you, but he wouldn't lie to you.

"Get some coffee," I said. "We'll talk."

Vinnie nodded and opened the car door.

"If you get donuts, get extra. The dog likes them."

Vinnie looked at me without comment for a moment and closed the car door. By the time he came back, I had finished the comics and folded the paper and put it on the floor in the backseat. He had two cups of coffee and a bag of donuts.

Pearl wagged her tail and nosed at the bag.

"Can you control this fucking hound?" Vinnie said.

"No," I said.

He handed me the bag and I took out a donut and broke it in two and gave Pearl the smaller half. I took a bite of my half and pried the cover off the fresh coffee. It had been a rainy fall, and it was raining again. Market Street was a bright wet black. The traffic was sporadic and slow. And the parking lot at the discount lumberyard across the street was nearly empty except for one guy in an emergency slicker he'd made from a green trash bag, tying a piece of surplus plywood to the roof of a ten-year-old Subaru wagon.

"I been trying to figure this out," Vinnie said.

Pearl was gazing at the cinnamon donut Vinnie was holding. Her head moved as his hand moved.

"Dog's supposed to get a bite," I said.

"Fuck," Vinnie said, and broke off a small piece and fed it to her gingerly. He wiped his hand on his pants leg.

"I been trying to figure out where I stand in this between you and Gerry and Joe," Vinnie said.

"Un huh."

"Joe figures the only way Gerry's ever going to be a man is to face up to something bad—"

"Which is me," I said.

"Which is you," Vinnie said. He trolled the coffee cup a little to stir it, and had a sip. "To face up to you and to win."

"Except he won't win," I said.

"No," Vinnie said. "He won't. He ain't that kind of man."

"More than one kind," I said.

"Maybe, but Joe don't know that."

"Neither does Gerry," I said.

"No, he don't, and it fucks him up worse than you'd think anything could."

"You think he'll try?" I said.

"Yeah."

Vinnie broke off another small bit of donut and fed Pearl.

"Joe want you to help him?" I said.

"No." Vinnie stared out the window down the nearly empty street at the car wash standing idle, looking better in the rain, like everything seemed to. "No. It's family. You saw him send me out when he come to talk with you. Him and Gerry."

"I always kind of figured you were family, Vinnie."

Vinnie shrugged. "Well, I ain't. I been with Joe since I was seventeen. I was a jerk kid, but I was willing, you know? Nobody too tough. No alley too dark. Nobody too special for me to kill. I was always willing. I was never scared."

"Always for Joe," I said.

"I never had nobody else."

"So Gerry will come after me without backup?" I said.

Vinnie shook his head. "Joe'll send him out alone," Vinnie said. "I know Joe. Because he thinks that's the only way the kid can ever be anything but a sleazy little punk. But he knows he's no good, and he don't want something to happen to him. So he'll come too. He'll trail along behind to protect the kid."

"So if he's right, he'll undercut the kid even if I don't
kill him."

"Yeah. Joe loves the kid."

"So he'll either get him killed or he'll take away his
victory by not letting him do it alone."

"Yeah."

"Kid would be better off if Joe didn't love him."

"Yeah."

We were quiet. The rain sliding down the front windshield made the traffic lights fluid and impressionistic at
the intersection.

"The thing is," Vinnie said, "Joe ain't that good anymore."

I nodded and drank some coffee and took another piece
of donut and shared it with Pearl.

"He gets involved," Vinnie said, "and you'll clip him
too."

"If I have to," I said.

"I thought about taking you out for him," Vinnie said.

"Which is why you've been following me."

"Yeah."

"But if you do that," I said, "Joe will never forgive you.
Because you ruined it for his kid."

"Yeah."

"Easier, wasn't it," I said, "when some guy gave Joe
trouble all you had to do was go round and drill him."

Vinnie drank a little more coffee, staring at the rain. He
took another donut, and automatically gave Pearl a piece,
and ate the rest.

"I'm getting out," Vinnie said. "I'm quitting Joe."

I stared at him. I couldn't think of anything to say.

"You do what you gotta do," Vinnie said. "You have to

kill them, you have to kill them. I won't come around asking you about it. I'm out of it."

He drank the last of his coffee. He took the final donut out of the bag and looked at it for a moment, then put the whole donut back for Pearl to take. Which she did. Vinnie opened the door and put one foot out onto the ground.

I put out my hand. Vinnie took it. We shook hands. Then he got out and closed the door. He turned the collar up on his raincoat and walked back to his car and got in. I saw the wipers start. The headlights went on. And he drove away. From the backseat Pearl nosed at my ear. Her breath smelled of donuts.

35

With a pronounced limp, I was walking Pearl on a leash in the Public Gardens when Gerry made his try. He came across the footbridge over the Swan Boat Pond with the low morning sun shining on his left, making his shadow splash long and peculiar across the railing toward Beacon Street. He was walking stiffly, and very slowly, and he held his right hand close in against his right thigh. I stopped near the monumental statue of George Washington and took the Browning out from under my arm.

"You're not going to like this," I said to Pearl, "but there's nothing to be done."

I was surprised at the way he came. I had thought he'd try to shoot me in the back. People on their way to work didn't pay much attention to the fact that there were two men with guns approaching each other in the Public Gardens. It wasn't quite that they didn't see the guns. It was that, hurrying toward work on a pretty morning, they didn't really record them.

The flower beds had been banked for the winter, and the swan boats stored up on the dock. But the grass was still green from the rainy autumn, and the trees, without leaves now, still arched elegantly. The leafless twigs looked lacy in the morning light.

Pearl was pointing a pigeon near the base of the statue.

Gerry kept coming, mechanical, almost spectral, somehow less than human, a disjointed, clumsy, fantastic figure in the bright new day; driven by things I could guess at but would never know, he came.

And behind him from a big car double-parked on Charles Street his father came, wearing a big loose overcoat, holding something under it, hurrying with his head ducked a little and his shoulders hunched, the way people do when they are trying not to be noticed.

Pearl's pigeon flew away and Pearl glanced around at me, annoyed that I hadn't responded to her point. She saw, or maybe smelled, the gun and her ears flattened, and her tail went down.

"Hang on, babe," I said. "I don't like this either, but it will be over quick."

I made sure the leash was looped over my left wrist. I held the stem of the leash tightly in my left hand. Joe was maybe thirty yards behind Gerry. Gerry was in range. I should plug Gerry now so I'd have time to deal with Joe. If I let them both get up on me it was going to be harder.

Gerry kept coming. He moved as if his joints hurt and wouldn't bend properly. He was close enough so I could see his face, shrunk tight, the cords visible in his neck, tension bunching his narrow shoulders.

"Gerry," I said.

He shook his head and kept coming. As he came he raised the gun. It was an automatic, foreign maybe, a Beretta or a Sig Sauer. He held the gun straight out in his right hand as he walked, and hunched his head down a little to squint along the barrel.

For the first time people noticed. They scattered soundlessly. No one spoke, or yelled, or screamed, or sighed. They moved. Behind Gerry, Joe rushed slowly forward. If Gerry could do it, he didn't want to spoil it by interfering. If Gerry didn't do it, he wanted to be able to save him. I had other things to think about, but for a moment I knew how awful this must be for both of them.

Then Gerry fired and missed, as somehow he would have to miss. I'm not sure he even saw me over the gunsight, and I turned sideways and brought the Browning up carefully. Lurching as he was, trying to shoot while coming at me, Gerry didn't have much chance of hitting me. I sighted with my left eye, along the barrel of the gun, and let the middle of his chest sit on the small white dot on the front sight. I cocked it with my thumb and took a careful breath, and dropped the sight and shot Gerry in the right knee. He went down as if his legs had been scythed. Behind him his father screamed, *"Gerry, Jesus Christ, Gerry!"* and flung himself forward on top of his son, shielding him with his body. The sawed-off shotgun he'd been holding under his coat clattered onto the hottop walkway and skittered maybe six feet.

"My leg," Gerry said in amazement. "My leg, Papa—he shot me in the leg."

"Don't shoot him," Joe was saying, quite softly. "Don't shoot him."

I dropped to one knee, still holding the Browning, and put my arm around Pearl. She was shaking and trying to run at the same time she was trying to climb into my lap.

"I had to shoot him, Joe." I said. "I won't shoot him again if I don't have to."

214

Gerry began to cry. It was shock mostly. It was too soon probably for the pain to start. In the distance I could hear a siren. If Gerry were lucky there'd be an ambulance soon and somebody could give him a shot before it got bad. Joe was crouching on the sidewalk beside Gerry, patting his face and smoothing his hair.

"You're going to be okay," he said. "I hear the ambulance. It's going to be okay. You're not bleeding bad."

"Papa, I'm scared."

"You'll be okay," Joe said. "You're going to be okay."

Pearl was quieter, but she leaned very hard against me as I knelt beside her. At what probably seemed to them a safe distance, people had stopped and were gazing back at us. The sirens were louder.

Joe looked at me. We were both kneeling.

"You could have killed him," Joe said.

I nodded.

"It was a hell of shot with somebody chopping away at you."

"Hard to shoot while you're walking fast, and scared," I said.

Joe nodded and looked down at Gerry. Gerry was sniffling, trying not to cry, shifting as the shock began to wear off and the first hint of pain began to come.

"He's my only kid," Joe said.

"Kid doesn't belong in this business, Joe," I said.

"I thought he could learn," Joe said. "If he doesn't take it, who does?"

"Get him into something else, Joe. Landscaping, chorus girls, something. If he takes over the business, he won't last a month."

"Vinnie's gone," Joe said.

"I know."

"Vinnie coulda run it."

"I know."

Gerry moaned. "It's starting to hurt, Papa," he said. "It's starting to hurt like a bastard."

Joe, hunched on his knees, bent awkwardly over with the stiffness of age, and pressed his face against Gerry's.

"It's gonna be okay," he said.

"I came for him, Pa," Gerry said. "I wasn't afraid of him."

"I know," Joe said. "I know."

The sirens were right on us now, and the first prowl car came swerving up the walkway and halted beside us. The two cops in it got out with guns drawn but not leveled. Behind them came another one. On Arlington Street, near the entrance to the Public Gardens a big yellow and white ambulance parked, its lights flashing as an un-marked police car swung out around it and came in be-hind the two prowl cars.

"He's not a shooter, Joe," I said.

"He ain't like me," Joe said. "He's like his mother."

"Let him be, Joe. If he comes after me again I might have to kill him. If it's not me, it'll be somebody else. He's not a shooter, Joe. Let him try to be something else. Keep him alive."

"Yes," Joe said and kept his face pressed against Gerry's until the EMTs showed up.

36

The ambulance took Gerry to the hospital. Joe and two detectives went with him. I knew one of the detectives who stayed with me, a guy named J. Clay Lawson, who was once a cop in Las Vegas before he got serious. He let me take Pearl home and then he and I spent the day with Quirk and Belson and a guy from the DA's office in the homicide squad room.

When they were through discussing my failings, albeit temporarily, I went home and had dinner with Susan, which I cooked, even though she'd wanted to, because I needed to do something.

"You're all right," Susan said.

"Yes."

"You want to talk about it?"

"No."

"Okay."

We ate chili and corn bread in front of the fire in my apartment and drank beer with it. Even Susan drank beer with chili, though she didn't drink much.

"Paige called me today," she said. "She said Paul seems—how did she put it?—'remote,' since he came back to New York."

I nodded, staring at the fire.

"Finding his mother made it more complicated, not less. He thought it would make it less."

"You probably can't help him with that," Susan said.

"I know."

Pearl lay in front of the fire, looking back frequently to check the status of chili and corn bread. Susan ate a small forkful of chili and nibbled the edge of a small piece of corn bread. With the chili and corn bread we had some corn relish that Susan and I had made as an experiment last Labor Day.

Outside it had begun to rain again. The sunny morning had been an illusion.

"You told me how you started to cook," Susan said. "You never have said why you like it."

"I like to make things," I said. "I've spent a lot of my time alone, and I have learned to treat myself as if I were a family. I give myself dinner at night. I give myself breakfast in the morning. I like the process of deciding what to eat and putting it together and seeing how it works, and I like to experiment, and I like to eat. There's nothing lonelier than some guy alone in the kitchen eating Chinese food out of the carton."

"But cooking yourself a meal," Susan said, "and sitting down to eat it with the table set, and maybe a fire in the fireplace . . ."

"And a ball game on . . ."

"And a half bottle of wine, perhaps."

I nodded.

Susan smiled, the way she does when her face seems to get brighter.

"You are the most self-sufficient man I have ever known," she said.

"Except maybe Hawk," I said. "Hawk's so self-sufficient he doesn't need to eat."

"Perhaps," Susan said.

"It's like carpentry," I said. "I get pleasure out of making things."

"But not in groups," Susan said.

I thought about that for a moment.

"True," I said.

"You like to read," Susan said. "You like to cook, you like to lift weights, and jog, and do carpentry, and watch ball games. Do you like to go to the ballpark?"

"I like to go to the park sometimes, keep in touch with the roots of the game, I suppose. But mostly I prefer to watch it on television at home."

"Alone?"

"Yes. Unless you develop an interest."

Susan didn't even bother to comment on that possibility.

"See what I mean?" she said.

"Autonomy?" I said.

"Yes. You only like things you can do alone."

"There are exceptions," I said.

"Yes. And I know the one you're thinking of. Me excepted, your interests are single."

"True," I said.

"You couldn't stand being a member of the police force."

"No. I hate being told what to do."

"You certainly do," Susan said.

"I'm cute though."

"You're more than cute," Susan said. "You're probably peerless, there's a kind of purity you maintain. Everything is inner-directed."

"Except the part about you," I said.

"Except that."

"That's a large part."

"I know that. Sometimes I'm sort of startled at the, ah, honor I'm the one you let in."

"Might be something of a burden sometimes, being the only one."

"No," Susan said. "It's never a burden. It is to be taken seriously, but it is never burdensome."

"You are the woman in my life," I said.

"Surely not the first."

"No, not in that sense," I said. "But remember how I grew up."

Susan nodded. "All men."

"Yeah, all men. It seemed right. Even looking back it seems right. It doesn't seem as if anything was missing. I knew women and had girlfriends, and so did my father and my uncles; but home was male."

Susan looked around the apartment. Pearl made a small snuffing sound in front of the fire and lazed over onto her side.

"And that is still the case," Susan said.

"No," I said, "no more. This is where I live. But home is where you are."

Susan smiled at me. "Yes," she said. "We are home."

We put plates down for Pearl, and cleared the table and put the pre-lapped dishes in the dishwasher.

"I need dessert," I said.

"You certainly do," Susan said.

"There's nothing here," I said.

"What would you like?"

"Pie?"

"Where is the closest source?" Susan said

Which is how we ended up walking close together underneath a multicolored golf umbrella along Arlington Street and into the Public Gardens where, so lately, I had been with the Broz family.

"Place near the Colonial Theater," I said, "will sell you pie and coffee almost any time of the day or night."

"Mark of an advanced civilization," Susan said.

She had her arm through mine and her head against my shoulder as we walked through the rain, sheltered by the umbrella. She had her cobalt raincoat on, the collar turned up around her black hair. The lining of the raincoat was chartreuse, and where the collar was up and open at the neck it showed in gleaming contrast under the streetlights. We walked past the statue of Washington, facing up the Commonwealth Avenue Mall across Arlington Street. If there were bloodstains on the sidewalk, the rain had washed them away, or masked them with its gleaming reflections. The garden was empty on a rainy night, and still, except for the sound of the rain. There was light from the lampposts. And the ambient city noise made the silence of the garden seem more complete. In the Swan Boat Pond the ducks were huddled under their feathers among the rocks along the shore of the lagoon.

The Common was ahead, across Charles Street, where once the inner harbor had washed against the foot of Beacon Hill, before they dumped in all the landfill and created the Back Bay and pushed the sea back into the harbor and the basin of the Charles River. Once it had really been a back bay, a mix of river water and ocean into which the oldest part of Boston had pushed like the bulge in a balloon.

Across Charles Street, not waiting for the light because there was no traffic, we moved uphill gently, across the Common, angling toward Boylston Street where an all-night diner served things like pie, and coffee in thick white mugs with cream and sugar. The winding walkways that bent through the Common were shiny with rain, and the unleaved trees glistened blackly. Around the lamps there formed a dim halo of mist that softened the light and made it elegant. To our left Beacon Street went up the hill to the State House, its gold dome lit and visible from everywhere, its Bulfinch front pretending that what went on inside were matters of gravity and portent. The wind that had, in the late afternoon, slanted the rain in hard as I left police headquarters, had died with the daylight, and the rain, softer now, came down in near perfect silence.

There were no pigeons about the Common at this hour, no squirrels. There was a fragrant bum sleeping on one of the benches under some tented cardboard which shed most of the rain. And, further along, several others slept, or at least lay still, wrapped in quilts and sleeping bags and newspapers.

"Are you in a pie reverie?" Susan said.

"Cherry," I said. "Blueberry, apricot."

"No apple?"

"Rarely do they make good apple pie," I said. "Usually they don't cook the apples enough, and sometimes, too often, they leave, yuk, some of the core in there. Cherry is my favorite."

"And coffee?"

"Decaf," I said sadly.

"How embarrassing," Susan said.

"Caffeine, like youth," I said, "is wasted on the young."

We passed the ancient burial grounds, the little cemetery near Boylston Street where earnest Calvinists had settled into the ground, relaxed at last.

"Are you planning on pie?" I said.

"No," Susan said. "I think I'll just have a cup of hot water, with lemon, and watch you."

"You walked a mile in the rain to drink hot water?"

"To be with you," she said. "You're better than pie."

And I turned under the umbrella and embraced her with my free arm and pressed my mouth against hers and held her hard against me and smelled her perfume and closed my eyes and kissed her for a long time in the still rain, and even after we stopped kissing, I held on to her and we stood together in the dark under the umbrella, until finally I didn't need to hold on anymore, and it was time to go across the street and have some cherry pie. Which we did.